CAPTIVE
DESIRE

CAPTIVE DESIRE

ROBIN LOVETT

Entangled Publishing, LLC
2614 South Timberline Road
Suite 105, PMB 159
Fort Collins, CO 80525
rights@entangledpublishing.com

Scorched is an imprint of Entangled Publishing, LLC.

Edited by Tracy Montoya
Cover design by Cover Couture
Cover photography by Shutterstock /Arthur-studio10 ;
Depositphotos/Timbrk; Depositphotos/JohanSwanepoel;
Shutterstock/ Conrado

Manufactured in the United States of America

First Edition November 2018

entangled
scorched

Chapter One

Assura

It hurts—my body burns like it's on fire. I am agony.

Through the haze of pain, I see it. The first break in the trees since I crash-landed on this godsforsaken planet a week ago. I stumble from the jungle, my vision blurring.

Days of no one and nothing but this fever scorching through my veins. It's not a normal fever. I don't know how it's possible, but it makes me want and think of nothing but sex. I'm pulsing between my legs, craving to be fucked, feeling I will burst into flames if I'm not. I'm chafed between my legs from days of giving myself orgasms, trying and failing to relieve the lust raging in my veins, the side effect of some gaseous poison in the air.

I fall to my knees on a stretch of runway. I see buildings, starships, people. Civilization. I start to shake. I can't hold myself up. My will to keep fighting is gone.

I crumble to the ground, writhing in pain.

Voices sound all around me. Whoever is here…they may

be friendly, they may be my enemy, but I'm not capable of finding out.

I'm too exhausted to open my eyes, but someone touches me, cradles my head in their lap. I want to scream at them to stop. I can't bear to be touched; being held hurts like a thousand knives scraping my too-sensitive skin.

"What is your name, human?" The deep voice resonates with a trace of revulsion. My humanity is something he doesn't like. By his accent, heavy on the consonants and slow on the vowels, I think I know what language he speaks. Which means I likely know why he would hate me on sight.

I open my eyes and see nothing but his face—his golden face. His skin shimmers metallic in the sunlight, and the sharp planes of his features glint in its rays. The darker gold waves of his hair nearly sparkle, and his eyes shine a blue so bright, I swear I'm looking into a cloudless sky. He looks divine, like some sort of god descended from a faraway mythical paradise.

I recognize his species. He is Ssedez, and I wonder he hasn't killed me; one of his warriors already tried several days ago. But I'm a special kind of soldier, the kind that's not so easily killed. They attacked and destroyed our ship. I was stabbed, given a wound that still festers in my side. It's his fault I'm stranded on this planet and had to spend a week alone wandering its toxic jungle.

But for a reason I don't understand, this Ssedez is not attacking me, and I have no energy to fight him anyway.

"Your name," he demands again.

There's a ring of authority to his tone, and it makes me want to do as he says. If I'm going to survive, I need medical attention. I need his help. "Assur," I answer, but the word twists my stomach. It's what my commanding officers called me. It's not my real name. "Assura," I correct.

The burn, the fire, surges in my body again, and I can't

stop the cry of agony escaping my lips. I fist my hands against the urge to touch myself. It'll only hurt. Breathing the air of this planet infects me with an endless and unquenchable need for release, even past the point of injury or exhaustion.

I feel something swelling under my head in his lap. I turn my cheek and feel a long column of rigid flesh hardening behind the leather of his uniform—his cock.

I don't give a shit if he's my enemy. I'm so desperate to relieve the flames torching my insides, I'll do anything to be fucked, to have him thrusting that into my starved body.

I claw at his thighs, bite my teeth at the leather shielding him from me. I'm moaning hungry sounds and hallucinating about him fiercely pouring his come in my mouth. Then, something is put in my mouth, a tube. It's not a cock, but I'm so hungry for it, I suck on it like it is one. A creamy liquid pours from it into my mouth. I swallow it, starved and praying it will satisfy me, not caring if it's poison meant to kill me. Dying would be better than enduring this any longer.

But it's not poison.

It slides down my throat and cools me from the inside out. The feeling spreads through my chest and into my limbs. I go motionless, the burn blissfully fading away. My breath is heavy with relief, and I glance up into the Ssedez's face again and whisper, "Thank you."

His ethereally blue eyes blanch in surprise and don't look away. He examines my face, and he must see something he likes. Heat infuses his expression, desire contrary to anything that should be possible for a Ssedez to feel for a human.

Exhaustion overtakes me. My eyes fall closed, and he lifts me. My cheek rests on his wide chest, and his inhumanly strong arms support my weight. His voice rumbles beneath my ear, his skin cool against the heat still fading from me.

The contours of his muscles are hard and chiseled beneath my hands. The feel of him is alien, too, smoother than human, refined like aluminum, not forgiving like human flesh. His bare skin has the characteristic impenetrability of his species. He's not soft, and he's cooler in temperature. I burrow my overheated body into his, blissfully chilled by his skin. I shudder, wondering if he's like that everywhere.

All I can do now is rest against him, but later, I will find out. The fever may have faded, but the desire that was ravaging my body still echoes in my core like a dull murmur.

When I wake, I hope he's there to fuck me.

Chapter Two

GAHNIN

I loathe the sight of her.

I touch her because I have orders from my commander to care for her. No other reason could motivate me to do so. And so I am forbidden from killing this Assura.

She cries sounds of erotic need and writhes in my lap. And unbidden and indisputably, my body reacts to her.

I gape at her in shock and search myself again to see if it is true.

As disgusting as it to me...

I want her.

It is an untenable response. Something that defies every desire I have had since her kind, the humans of the Ten Systems Empire, killed my mate in a brutal war against the Ssedez a century ago. My existence, the drive of every part of my life, has been for vengeance. And yet, I feel a desire that defies my decades of hatred, a need that interrupts what was to be two centuries of mourning for my lost mate a century too early.

I want to satisfy this human, to relieve the planet-driven lust that is paining her. To slake the same lust that is brimming within me, filling and hardening me with a foreign desire for a human that is as unwelcome to me as nails in my heart.

I hold her head, so she cannot rub and provoke my arousal. Tears of agony drip from her eyes, and her nails dig into my forearms with such ferocity, if I had vulnerable human skin, she would draw blood.

But I am Ssedez, and my skin is invulnerable to her pathetic attempts to free herself. What is more shocking, her nails imbedded in and scraping over my skin feel... pleasurable, as though if I could, I would let her do this to my entire body, and it would provoke my craving for her only further.

It is intolerable. For me to feel such things at the touch of a human is revolting. I don't care if my commander Oten has formed the Attachment, a sacred Ssedez mating bond that is both biological and emotional, with this Assura's General Nemona. It matters not that Nemona and Assura, along with all the humans aboard their ship, the *Origin*, are in rebellion against our mutual enemy, the Ten Systems. I agree with Oten that it was a mistake to attack the *Origin*, causing it to crash-land on this planet, and that we must make amends by helping these rebels. I'm aware it is my duty to care for Assura, but no amount of duty can cure my impulse to hate her. I am still appalled at my own body's traitorous attraction to her.

It is undoubtedly due to this planet, Fyrian. The Fellamana, the native species here, say the fever-like state of intense arousal both the humans and Ssedez have experienced here, a condition they call the *desidre,* is caused by toxins in the atmosphere. They gave me an antidote on landing here, but it must not be working for me. Assura needs the antidote, too. Perhaps it will work on her.

"Assist her!" I shout at the medical attendant. I'm surrounded by the medical team of Fellamana who met us here on their landing platform. My commander left on our ship, leaving me and a team of Ssedez here on the planet Fyrian to establish diplomatic relations with the Fellamana.

One of the Fellamana responds in a language I don't understand.

The male Fellamana beside her, whom they introduced as Koviye, seems to translate my words for her. She registers understanding and rushes forward, pulling a round tube containing the liquid antidote from her bag and placing it between Assura's lips.

The human sucks on it greedily, her cheeks hollowed, and I am besieged by a fantasy of my cock in its place, of her soft pink lips wrapped around my hard, gold flesh, pleasurable moans vibrating from her as I satiate her mouth. I grimace and will the image away, pretending I never saw it. She is a forsaken human.

She relaxes, her body soaking in the relief of the antidote. Her eyelids flutter open, and she whispers, "Thank you," in a rasping voice. I am enraptured by the swelling of gratitude in her eyes.

I want her to give me that look after I have driven her body to climactic ecstasy.

She closes her eyes again, and I am grateful. These lustful notions about her that are permeating my brain must stop now.

Two more Fellamana, their iridescent robes swirling about their legs, come forward with a stretcher, intending to transport Assura to the hospital, I presume. But I shove them off. "I will carry her."

It is unnecessary. Beyond the requirements of my duty, but for a reason I do not want to contemplate, I cannot let anyone else hold her. I lift her in my arms, cradling her to my chest. She drifts into unconsciousness, leaving me embroiled in confusion at myself and clinging to the assertion that it is only this place making me want to touch her.

It cannot be because I actually desire a human.

In the hospital, they uncover an infected wound in her side. It elicits my first feelings of guilt toward this woman. The wound was undoubtedly sustained in the battle aboard her ship. One of my fellow Ssedez warriors stabbed her.

The best I can do to make amends, as Oten has commanded, is help her heal.

The Fellamana medics must reopen her wound to treat the infection. Assura is still unconscious, but I hold her shoulders down in case the procedure awakens her.

I press her shoulders firmly into the mattress that automatically molds itself to her proportions and weight. "Ready," I say and Koviye translates. The medic injects her with an anesthetic then makes the first cut into Assura's side.

She jerks awake and tries to fight me. Terror contorts her features. She does not know where she is or what is happening.

"They are treating your wound," I say in her language, not in my own.

She grits her teeth and grips my arms but does not fight me. She stares at my face, and I give her more words of comfort. "It will be over soon."

Our gazes lock, and I do not know what to call the communication between us. It is as though a temporary truce is met.

The medic finishes, and with the procedure over, Assura slips back into unconsciousness.

I sit in a chair by her door. Day and night.

Only because I communicated with Commander Oten, and he reiterated his order for me to watch over Assura. He may be on a ship en route to our home world, but I must still obey his word as law, given our military chain of command. He is a fair leader, and I trust him. He is on a mission with his new mate, General Nemona, to get supplies that may repair her ship the *Origin,* which crash landed not far from here after we destroyed their reactor in our attack.

My entire life, I thought of humans as untrustworthy and intrinsically selfish by nature. Humans have warred among their own kind from the dawn of their existence. They cling to violence as a way of life, and their need to conquer other species without mercy is embedded in their genes. Now that my Commander Oten has mated with one, I am faced with the truth that not all humans are thus, but merely the Ten Systems.

It confuses every instinct I have to be here, guarding a human whom I have been trained to kill at first sight.

Which is what we did when the *Origin* entered our home planet's airspace. Their ship bore the markings of a Ten Systems warship. We did not know that Nemona and her crew had escaped the empire using one of its ships. It was the first Ten Systems vessel we had seen in decades.

I've never actually met a human before, though I have been conditioned by my military training and my wartime experiences to hate them.

Everything about Assura is like the human enemy I was trained to kill, from her hair, dark as midnight lying over her shoulders, to her pert little mouth, pinched with pain. Though her limbs are molded with strength as fine as that of my warriors, her skin is something I have never felt before.

I know her language. I studied it for years in my warrior's training, in my lifelong study of our human enemies from the

Ten Systems Empire. But when she writhes and moans in her sleep, she doesn't communicate with words—but the noises she makes seem to me like sexual want. The sound she makes is throaty and resonant and sends a bolt of lust through my body. It is something I should not be able to feel—not so soon after my mate's death. It's been only a hundred years. According to our traditions, I'm supposed to wait another hundred more before my desire for another reawakens, and certainly not for one of the species who killed a million Ssedez and attempted our genocide a century ago. At that time, we feared our annihilation by the Ten Systems so severely, we destroyed our home planet in a catastrophic bombing to fake the extinction of our race. Our plan succeeded, and we've kept sanctuary on a planet unknown to the Ten Systems since. No matter what my commander orders, it doesn't change the fact that the Ssedez lost everything because of humans.

Assura stretches her long limbs in wakefulness, her firm breasts and rounded hip outlined by the thin sheet. Bright daylight streams through the floor-to-ceiling windows and onto her bed, and her eyes open, full of all the desire emanating from her.

Her expression is still lax from fatigue, but her gaze is fully aware. "What's your name, Ssedez?" She mirrors my question from yesterday, and her voice comes out stronger than it did then. It sends a tremor through my limbs. I have to force myself to focus, to not stare at her lips forming the words.

I sit forward. "I am Gahnin."

She breathes in and out slowly, as though her tired mind requires time to speak. "You attacked our ship."

"Yes."

"Why are you here?" Her tone is all skepticism and confusion.

"Because I was commanded to watch over you."

"Why? By whom?" Her soft brown eyes slant, narrowing on me. She does not yet believe I am a friend. Good, she should not.

"My commander charged me to watch over you until they return. Your General Nemona, she is his new mate."

"She?" She eases upward in her bed, growing more confused. "Your translation is wrong. General Nem is male. And he would never mate with a Ssedez."

I sneer at her insinuation that it is my error. "I speak your language perfectly. Nemona knew you. She wept when I showed her the image of you on the communication vid. She believed you dead."

Her eyes widen in confusion and surprise. "Wait, a Ssedez mated with...her?" At least in this our reactions are similar.

"It is hard to believe that one of my kind would Attach to a human, but yes, it has happened."

She shakes her head, then grabs it like it hurts. "Am I your prisoner?"

"I am in charge of you."

She gives a low growl. "No one is in charge of me." She pushes back the sheet and is startled to find that underneath she is naked. "Where's my uniform?"

I mean to turn away, but the covering slides down to reveal her breasts. I glimpsed her body while the doctors treated her, but I forced myself not to look.

I cannot now.

Her skin looks soft as velvet, and her nipples are round and ripe. And the unabating lust steaming through my veins roars within me. I would take her in my mouth. I would see her beneath me. I would spread her legs and see what she looks like in the place where she is meant to take my cock into her.

"Oh gods!" She is staring at me. Staring at my mouth.

What is...

Ah, *fuck*.

I close my eyes. Cringing. She cannot be staring at what I think she is staring at.

But I know she is. I can feel them, elongating in my mouth, the tips pressing into my lower lip. I touch them to make sure I'm not imagining this.

I feel them, fully extended—my fangs. This cannot be happening. I race to the mirror by the door to make sure.

There they are. Two inches of white tooth, twins. I have not seen them in a hundred years. That they have descended, biologically, means only one thing…

A crash sounds behind me.

I whirl, and Assura is stumbling from her bed toward the door. She's naked and unstable on her feet.

"Wait." I reach for her, not wanting her to fall and hurt herself.

"Don't touch me." She tries to push me away, but her legs give out, weaker than she expected. I catch her before she hits the floor.

She is in my arms, pressed against my chest, her skin as smooth beneath my hands as it was before. More so. Like the texture and delicacy of moonlight.

She fights against my hold but for only an instant.

Her gaze, level with my shoulders, traces over my bare chest, and she stills. I have no need of a shirt. Ssedez do not wear them; our natural armor protects us from injury and weather.

Her fingers press and feel my pecs, like she's curious.

She makes that sound…

That moan filled with a longing so thick, it comes from deep within her. She molds her breasts to my chest, grabs my shoulders, and moves against me.

I cannot help it. I slide my hand up her neck to her nape, sinking my fingers into her silken hair. It is as thrilling to touch as I imagined it would be. I cradle her head in my hand, and her name slides from my lips, "Assura," laced with more longing than I should ever reveal.

It is insanity to feel these things for her—to want to touch her. But I cannot stop my bodily desire any more than I can shut down my nervous system.

She lifts her head, her gaze locked on my mouth. The long delicate column of her neck is exposed, and, unable to resist, I lower my nose to her throat. I inhale her scent—like sweet fruit and sensual heat. The need to penetrate her, to sink my fangs into her vein, aches in my gums. To bite her would enact a mating ritual that, among my people, is as ancient as the Ssedez.

I graze her skin, scratching the tips of my fangs over her neck.

She clings to my head, as though she wants me to bite her.

She has no idea that the need in me is like a tidal force—a carnal instinct born of my body's awakened desire to Attach to someone. It goes beyond desire. It is a primal craving, as though I will suffer and die if I do not give her what is dripping from my fangs. The venom is a rare gift. The pleasure it would inject her with, the ecstasy it would flow into every corner of her body... I want to share it with her.

I shudder, banish the need.

No matter how I want it, to give her the sacred venom would be a sacrilege to the traditions of my people. It is meant for only a lifelong mate.

And she will never be that.

No gods forsaken human ever could be.

It is against everything I dedicated my life to.

But the knowledge that I hate her and her kind does not penetrate my lust. Desire surges over my loathing, smothering it. The hatred is still there, underneath.

But the desire to make her come eclipses it, for now.

"Please," she begs, pressing my head to her neck. Her leg climbs mine, and she undulates her hips against me.

She is mindless for me. This lust that pours through me in this place, she feels it, too.

I may not be able to give her my venom, but I can give her the pleasures her own body is capable of.

She presses the apex of her thighs where my cock is as hard and erect as a metal blade. That's where she wants it. I do not know the anatomy of the human female.

But I will learn hers.

I back her into the bed behind us. She leans against it, and I trail my fingers down her hip, treasuring the feel of her skin. I reach a patch of hair, and it surprises me.

I cannot help it. I have to look down. This is something new to me. The Ssedez do not have hair, except on our heads. But the sight of it—the springy dark curls—incurs a growl from my chest. It makes me want to part it, to delve beneath it and discover what it hides from my view.

She clings to my arms and spreads her legs around my hips. "Don't stop."

I thread my fingers beneath the curls and press her—in the same place where she rubbed against me.

She groans and thrusts her hips against my hand.

I follow her rhythm, testing for what she likes, sensing what she needs. Soon, her mouth is open, and she's panting. "More."

She arches her hips and widens her thighs, exposing what lies beneath the curls.

Folds of wet and swollen flesh—a cunt of such erotic beauty, I go still, staring.

I have missed the female body. I did not know how much. I grow so hard, my cock painfully rubs against the fly of my leather uniform pants.

She does not have time for my reverence, though. She

moves my hand for me, snaking my fingertips beneath the hood of curls to a thickened nub—small but tender. She circles my fingers around it, the flesh moving and swelling at the pressure.

Her hand falls limp on my wrist, and she cries out an almost painful sound.

I worry a moment I have hurt her, but then she murmurs, "Yes."

Encouraged, I press harder and move my fingers in a fluid, circular pattern. Her breathing speeds, and I time my circles to her inhales, matching the waves of pleasure that seem to be flowing through her.

But it's not enough. There must be more to her, a place within her for my cock. But I don't want to stop doing what she likes.

With her holding herself up against me, I take my other hand and slide it through her folds, lower, searching, feeling.

The softness of her is almost more than I can bear. The wetness seething from within her is something I could bathe in. I cannot not imagine what it would feel like to bury myself in the warm slickness of her, how she would let me thrust within her, how the exquisite feel of her would let me move— fast, hard.

With my probing fingers, I stroke into an opening. The one hand still circling over the spot she likes, I sink a finger of my other hand within her. And reach no ending.

The limitless depth of her—it is unfathomable. It blows my thoughts and my imagination of what it would be like to fit inside her. She could take all of me.

That I have not been inside a female since *she* died at the hands of humans is not something I have time to contemplate. I shove the knowledge into a dark hole and pretend it isn't there.

I spread her with a second finger, testing her. It slides

in with ease, her dampness increasing the farther into her depths I go. Her cunt squeezes my fingers but relaxes, as though greedy for more. I sink another finger, then another, matching the size of my cock within her—to see if she can take it.

She throws her head back and whimpers. Her hips pump harder into my hands, and I am helpless not to imitate my cock with my fingers. I thrust my hand inside her—in and out, in time to my other circling hand.

Her body tenses; her hands go lax. She falls back on the bed, unable to hold onto me anymore.

She grips the bed covering. Her whole body thrusts into my hands, an instinct driven by a primitive need to climax.

Her breasts move as she does, and watching her face contort with bliss has me wishing I could fuck her. I'm hard and throbbing, but I want to watch her more than I want to take her that way—at least for now.

If I were to join her, I would miss the beauty of this. Of watching her orgasm. Of seeing her soak in and be overtaken by the satisfaction I'm giving her.

It begins within her, the climax. I feel it bunching inside her with the tensing of her around my fingers. I slow my movements, gradually, drawing it out. I do not want it to end. I do not want this to be over.

But she is too far gone, and the cries begin in her throat, ceaseless and primal. Her breathing stops, and she squeezes around me until it almost hurts my fingers. I love it, the eroticism of it stunning me.

Her climax peaks, and she lets go.

The ecstasy that storms over her face, followed by the release and total letting go of her body…it soothes something in me. It feeds a need, a desire to satisfy her.

And it exposes a crater inside me—an emptiness that I have been avoiding in my century of loneliness. I will not think of the wretched irony that is me finding this pleasure in a *human* female. I did not realize, though, how much I missed this—a female becoming mindless for what I make her feel.

I ease her through the aftershocks of the climax.

Her breasts pump up and down with rapid breaths, and her head and hands lie limp. Her knees collapse wide, and she does not open her eyes.

I may have taken too much out of her. She is still recovering from infection. The scar of her wound is still visible on her abdomen, a pinkened, jagged line. Perhaps I should not have given this to her.

But her breathing calms, and a blessedly blissful expression falls over her mouth. The worry and pain eases from her face in a way I have not seen from her yet.

I lift her and settle her head onto her pillow. I cover her with the sheet, and I am unable to resist caressing her cheek, her hands.

"Thank you," she whispers, just as I imagined she would yesterday. My breath stops. I made it come true. Her breath slows into an even, restful sleep—leaving me in shock.

I turn away from her, and my eyes stray to the glass wall—where anyone walking by in the hallway could have seen us. Hopefully, no one did.

I am...seething, no, overflowing with confusion and rife with horror at myself.

My fangs have not retracted. Which means only one thing.

My body thinks this human—one of the same kind who killed my first mate, the kind I have hated with everything in me for over a century—is my new mate.

Chapter Three

I sleep better than I have since I landed on this shit planet...
thanks to him.

My dreams are relaxing, easy. No more wandering
through the jungle afraid I'll never see anyone again. No
more dreams of where I came from or the horrific crimes I
was forced to commit under the orders of the Ten Systems.
Those days are over. I never have to obey that sickening
psychopath, General Dargule, again.

I dream of longing physically for satisfaction and of
my gold alien giving me everything I need. But even in my
dreams, I'm still tormented by the truth: *if he knew what
you'd done, he would kill you instead.*

It jerks me awake, and I see his chair is empty for the first
time.

It's good he's gone, so I'm not tempted to fuck him. I
never should've begged him to touch me. I've committed such
heinous crimes against one of his species—the unforgivable

type of crimes. It's wrong for me to be touching him, letting him help me, let alone heal me. Let alone give me orgasms!

And whether he finds out what I did or not, the Ten Systems humans waged a brutal war and attempted genocide against his people. It was a century ago, but they won't have forgotten how humans slaughtered their kind. Their lifespan is long, a thousand years or more. He may have even been alive when the war happened, unlike me at my twenty-eight years.

Humans and Ssedez are supposed to be enemies, despite the new truce between our two crews. I don't know why he chose to touch me. Or why I begged him to. It won't happen again.

Not because I didn't like it or want it because, well, shamelessly, obviously, I did. But it's an impossibility that never should've been possible. I've no idea what his motives are. He said he's in charge of me. He thinks I'm his prisoner. One of his warriors stabbed me.

I look down at the wound in my side—only a pink scar line remains. The Fellamana doctors removed the infection, and my body's bio-enhanced healing took over. Good. My bioengineering should have restored my depleted strength as well.

I have to get out of here and back to searching for my friends in the rebellion who may have survived the crash. If General Nem, who I still can't believe is female, survived, others did. These aliens may have helped me, but I have no idea what their further intentions are. I've got no desire to find out what the Ssedez plan for me.

But there's an ache low in my body that…

I groan and cover my face with my hands.

For real?

I can*not* still be horny. That orgasm he gave me yesterday was—I don't know how to describe it but…really good doesn't cover it.

I need to somehow ignore how swollen I am with craving

more, and not just an orgasm this time, but hot, sheet-clawing sex. I mentally sever my mind from physical sensation, a battle technique from my military training. It's possible to fight through most injuries as long as you can't feel the pain.

I have to focus. I need to get out of here and back to our ship. I saw the *Origin* crash-land; there have to be other survivors from the escape pods, like the one I landed in alone. The crash site is where they'll have gathered. Helping them, doing good deeds to try to make up for all the gruesome things I did to other species with the Ten Systems, is all that matters now. Getting back to my dearest friend Jenie is all I care about. If she survived.

Fear twists my stomach. She can't be dead. I refuse to entertain the possibility.

My training kicks in—awareness of the place, my surroundings.

The building is minimalist. There is no furniture in my room except for Gahnin's chair and my bed. All the walls are glass; everything is visible here. There is nowhere to hide.

Sneaking out is going to be a bitch, but I have to.

I don't even have time to get out of bed, to test how weak I still am. Gahnin walks in, and my heart starts racing like a speeder engaging its hyperdrive. The sight of him...gods, he is built for temptation. His eyes, those ethereally blue eyes, are hypnotizing in their clarity. He wears no shirt, his bulging chest and arms on display for everyone. I want to bite him, to dig my nails into that hard muscle. I can't help glancing lower on his body, following the trail of his tapered waist to his hips—and what hangs between them, behind the leather.

I am wet between my legs, and I have never had such an immediate response to someone, ever. The shock must be present on my face, the way I'm staring at him too obvious.

"It is the *desidre*," he rasps, his breath elevated, his eyes staring at my nakedness that I'd forgotten to cover up. "It is what causes this...reaction." He says the last word with a sickened disdain. He hates this as much as I do.

"But...I don't get it." I glance down at myself, disbelieving I can still be having these erotic responses. I can barely look at him without picturing his bare ass clenching as he thrusts into me with what is no doubt an enormous cock. "They gave me something to cure it."

"They tell me it relieves the fever that could kill you but not the whole lustful part of *desidre*. It's lessened, but it must still be fed."

I let out a heavy, frustrated breath. "So, going without sex isn't an option?"

"It appears not." He's rigid, every muscle bunched and strained. Gods, he's so fuckable, this is a crime. Why couldn't he have been any other species? Then this would not be a problem. It would be a pleasure.

I have to get out of here. But he's blocking the door. "Out of my way."

His shoulders stiffen. "You go nowhere. The Fellamana medics say you must feed the *desidre* before you are well enough to leave the hospital."

"To hell with that." I stand up, naked, but I don't care. I wobble a little, appalled that I have to brace my hand on the bed for balance.

His gaze wanders over my bare breasts before he forces his eyes to stay on my face. "We cannot continue our mission and leave for the Origin's crash site until you are well enough to accompany us."

I gape at him. "Who says I'm going with you?" I want to get back to my crew, but I don't want him with me.

"*I* say. My commander says. Your general says." He steps closer, attempting to intimidate me with his size, which is formidable. But I am not intimidated.

A snarl breaks from my teeth. "I'm going back, but I'm

going alone."

His brows scrunch in confusion, as though my statement makes no sense to him. "You have to take orders from someone. It is the foundation of military structure."

The more I talk to him, the faster I want to get away from him. "I'm not a Ten Systems soldier anymore. I'm in rebellion." I feel the strength returning to my muscles. I will it so. "I'm leaving. Move aside so I don't have to hurt you." He may be big, but I am quick and have outmaneuvered beings larger than him many times.

He almost laughs, crosses his arms, and blocks my view of the door. "No."

"No?" I step closer to him now, steadying myself for an attack.

He lowers his chin, his expression condescending. "I will not fight you. But I will keep you from hurting yourself."

I stalk toward him, uncaring that I'm naked. There are no clothes in this room, but I need no clothes to beat him. His condescension is my advantage. "Last chance."

He rolls his eyes and reaches for me. "You are still unwell. Please return to your bed."

I grab his throat and shove my thumb beneath his jaw where I know it hurts him. His eyes widen with surprise, and he chokes, "How did you—"

I shove my thumb deeper, cutting off his ability to speak. I've shocked him. There are very few ways to injure the Ssedez body. Their skin is basically armor. But I know all their weaknesses, thanks to my former job with the Ten Systems.

Gahnin's biological protective armor thickens—on instinct, his gold skin sprouts a diamond pattern, still the same tone as his skin. It's a genetic feature of the Ssedez, a second, armorlike layer of protection they pull out at will when they are threatened. He didn't do it before because he believed I couldn't hurt him. He knows now. His natural armor can't be penetrated with anything except fire. I can't break his bones, but there are weaknesses in the armor, sensitive places on him where pain can be inflicted.

Like where his head meets his spine, beneath his jaw. I dig in harder.

He flinches, and I smile, satisfied I've hurt him.

"Are you listening now?" I whisper with menace. I'm annoyed he's taller than me, so I can't intimidate him with my exceptional height, like I usually do human men.

He grips my forearm. "This is not a negotiation."

"That's what you think."

Too fast for him to defend himself, I knee him in the gut, which doesn't hurt him, but the force of it doubles him over. I seize his moment of weakness and knock his feet from under him.

Too easy.

But he doesn't disappoint. He rolls and lands on his feet with surprising agility that shouldn't be possible for someone of his size and muscular heft.

"This is how you want to do this?" he asks, perplexed. "In a hospital room?"

"Location is irrelevant. Getting away from you is." I will not be forced into leading this Ssedez to where my crew has crash-landed. They are vulnerable and recovering from a battle. The ship in tatters, their technologies weakened, they are in no state to be ambushed again by the Ssedez.

I don't care how talented his fingers are in the pleasure department. He's my enemy.

I charge him and slam him back against the wall. It's possible to knock a Ssedez unconscious, with the right amount of force to the correct spot of the head. I try it but fail.

He twists his arm around my shoulder and shoves my back into the wall.

I grunt. It forces the air from my lungs, and I see spots.

An alarm sounds in the hospital, a brutal *bong bong bong*.

My vision returns, and he's inches from my face—his fangs extended.

His massive, hard body cages mine, his thighs bracketing my hips, his pelvis anchoring me to the wall. I shudder and feel his cock digging into my belly through his leather.

Gods.

I'm not weak. I don't give in. I never lose.

But I want to.

I have a terrifying urge to surrender, to expose my vulnerable throat to him and let him penetrate me with his fangs. To let my body go limp beneath his pressure and become the soft vessel for him to unleash all his lust inside.

But I won't. No matter how much I want to.

He says something, the sound rumbling from his chest into mine. Except I can't understand what he's saying. The hospital alarm is too loud.

I have to deny this urge to give in and let him conquer me. I will not be his prisoner.

But the decision is robbed from me.

Shouting—in a language I don't understand—echoes through the room. Beings the likes of which I've never encountered pull Gahnin from me, restraining him.

Good. They'll assist me in getting away from him.

But they grab me, too.

The blaring alarm stops. My ears continue ringing, but I can hear voices again. I'm momentarily stunned by the aliens rushing into the room, too entranced by the sight of them to fight back.

Their complexions seem to glow, so clear, they're translucent. Iridescent ribbons of color wave beneath their skin, like their blood is visible. Each one of them is a different school of color, one greens and yellows, another orange and pink.

One male is a stunning array of blues and reds, his

features nearly as attractive as Gahnin's. "Koviye, it was a mistake," Gahnin says to him in my human language. "She is still unwell and does not understand."

Koviye responds in my language, his accent varying each word in pitch as though making it musical. "I don't create the laws, Gahnin. There are no exceptions. Violence is violence. Aggression is not tolerated." He says it with a slight smile, which he turns on me. "The punishment is not something to worry about, though. You'll probably enjoy it." He drops his smile abruptly with a thick warning. "If you cooperate."

"Who are you?" I ask, a little breathless. I've never seen their species before. I would remember.

Koviye sweeps me a polite bow with a flourish of his hand. "We are the Fellamana. We have healed you and clothed you and hoped you would receive our hospitality with gratitude." He steps closer, his gaze roaming my face with curiosity. "We have done nothing to provoke you." He doesn't seem offended, though, more like intrigued.

I test the hold of the guard restraining my arms behind my back. I could escape. It would require me to break his arm, though. Which I don't really want to do. "I am grateful to you for taking care of me. But I need you to let me go, now." I don't respond well to being trapped. I can't stand it for much longer.

"I'm afraid I can't." Koviye gives an amused smile as though this whole situation is entertaining. "You've broken our most sacred law."

"What law, Koviye?" Gahnin says, harshly, though he remains still. He's not fighting the restraint of the Fellamana. Which is a good plan for him, I guess. "Tell us so we can make amends. We are ignorant."

"No violence." Koviye spreads his arms like he's delivering wonderful news. "Your cultures are so barbaric, you don't know this. And so I will appeal to the elders to moderate your punishment. Though I can't make any promises." His mouth turns up at the corner like he's going to enjoy every minute of our "punishment."

"We did not know peace was so valued by the Fellamana," Gahnin says, diplomatically.

"Violence is never an option for the Fellamana. Fighting is a mark of unforgivable evil."

"Unforgivable?" I ask. This does not bode well.

"What is the punishment?" Gahnin asks.

Koviye's response is trivial. "Imprisonment. Without the *topuy*."

"What?!" Gahnin yells.

I swallow hard, praying this doesn't mean what I think it does. "What is the *topuy*?"

Koviye's compassionate smile is contrary to what his words mean. "It is the antidote to the *desidre*."

My blood roars in my ears like a beast on the defensive attack. The *desidre* fever I lived with in the jungle for days was *the* worst pain I have ever experienced. I have been through horrible things. I am no stranger to fatal injury. I've almost died in battle many times. Pain and I are old friends. But I have never experienced anything like the merciless *desidre*. Without the *topuy*, the burning will come back. Without the antidote to the *desidre*, I'll fall into the feverish lust I lived with in the jungle again.

No. Not happening.

I don't care that I'm still naked. At this moment, I don't care that what I should want most is to make peace with both of their species, making right the wrongs I have done. Not this time. I have to get out of here.

I wrench from the grip of the Fellamana trapping me. I hear a bone snap and a cry of agony, but I don't give a shit. I can't go back to living without the *topuy*. I've got to get to my crew.

"Assura, no!" Gahnin shouts at me. "Do not fight them."

I drop away, rolling across the floor, escaping the Fellamana guards without hurting them more.

Koviye touches my arm as I go by. "You're making it worse." His tone isn't a warning— just a statement of fact.

"Nothing is worse than going without the *topuy*," I spit.

"I will plead your ignorance of the no-tolerance laws," he says in my ear. "Hopefully it will be for only a day. But if you run, it will be longer."

Even a day is too long. I panic, frantic to never have to feel that torture of being without the *topuy*. I have to escape, in the hopes that our crew have manufactured their own version of the *topuy*. If our first aid equipment survived the crash, our shipboard doctors must have concocted something by now.

I dash into the hallway and run down the length of it. My muscles are not at full strength, but I have enough power to get away.

I search for a place to hide, but I'm surrounded by glass walls. It's dizzying. There are no dark corners, no doors to sneak through.

I'm visible to everyone. Medical staff shriek and dodge out of my way.

I'm trained for stealth. It's my specialty. But having nowhere to hide throws off every instinct I have.

I turn a corner and reach a dead end. The only place I see to conceal myself is behind a hospital bed in an unoccupied room. I sneak soundlessly inside—a plus to being barefoot.

I crouch behind the bed frame in time to hear the Fellamana guards in the hall, followed by Koviye's voice. "Assura, our security system is too advanced for you to leave without us knowing. Please reveal yourself."

I glance around me, searching for something. A weapon to fight back with, a piece of clothing to disguise myself. But there is nothing.

No objects, no drawers, no shelves, no levers, buttons, or

screens. I don't get it. How do these Fellamana work? There must be storage somewhere. But glancing through all the clear walls, there's no furniture except beds.

The only thing I can think is that it's all invisible.

My wits come back, and I see the flaws in my plan. I'll have to steal some *topuy*. It'll be no better than being their prisoner if I don't get some to take with me in my journey to my crew's crash site. I'll have to capture one of the healers and force them to get me some.

The thought turns my stomach. They've been so kind to me. I don't want to threaten them. I could get past the guards, but I will have to knock them out. I don't want to risk accidentally killing them.

"Assura," Gahnin's low voice resonates outside my room. "Let us work out a diplomatic compromise. We aim to be allies. Please do not make this bloody."

It's like he read my thoughts.

He's right.

The Fellamana are not my enemy. They are not guilty of war crimes—like the Ssedez for attacking my ship while it was on a peaceful mission. Or the Ten Systems, whose obsession with power has corrupted them to pursue domination or destruction of every new species they meet. My behavior is contrary to what I set out to do when I escaped.

The only thing the Fellamana are guilty of is wanting to maintain a peaceful society. Which is to be admired. Unlike me. The guilt over what I have done in my past rakes its ugly claws through my chest.

This was a mistake.

But I don't get a chance to make it right. In my distraction, someone sneaks up on me. I have no warning. Just the prick of a needle as it's injected into my neck.

Chapter Four

GAHNIN

They dress an unconscious Assura in a skintight suit of opaque white material, then transport us to another building. We are put into a cell, which is predictably made of glass.

There's nothing in it except two sleeping pads. There's not even a latch for the door we enter through. The door disappears when it closes.

I feel for the seams with my hands, and it's like they are gone or never existed. No indentation, no groove, just smooth glass.

Extraordinary.

Assura lies sleeping on the pallet they placed her on. It's far from the comfort of the ergonomic hospital bed she's been in the last two days.

I should have guessed the Fellamana were pacifists who protect their peace with rigid regulations. It was obvious. I was too distracted with my obsessive lust for Assura to notice.

Outside the glass wall, one of my warriors, Pvotton,

arrives with a Fellamana guard to escort him. With a press of the guard's finger on the glass, an opening forms in the window for us to communicate.

Pvotton's gold face is tight with suppressed amusement. "Get into some trouble, Gahnin?" he asks in our Ssedez language.

I respond with our words. It is a pleasure to not have to speak the Ten Systems language. "Some trouble with the human." I nod toward Assura.

He sighs but refrains from asking why or how. He would never doubt me. His gaze is curious, heavy with concern. He is aware of my personal vendetta against her kind; he knows what a torturous duty Commander Oten set for me to sit with her. "Do you want a reprieve? We could ask for you to be put in a separate cell. I will take your place."

His offer is one of such generosity, I cannot reject it without gratitude. "Your honor in giving me such a choice is well noted, and I thank you."

He inhales a hard breath. "I would do it for you." He glances around. "She will need service to feed the *desidre*. This duty should not fall to you. It is not part of what Oten intended."

I grit my teeth against my visceral rejection of letting anyone touch her but me. "It should not fall to you, either."

He misunderstands the aggression in my tone. "You are in danger of hurting her. I will procure your exchange to a separate cell." He turns to go, and desperation takes hold of me.

"No!" And to my shame, my fangs start to descend.

He glances back at me and, at seeing my fangs, gasps. He knows what it means. "Oh gods!" He rushes back to me, horror straining his features. "You must allow me to arrange your exchange. This *desidre* has confused your body." He glances around to be sure no one is listening and whispers harshly, "She cannot be your mate!"

"No, she cannot."

"I know it happened to Oten with his human, but for you…this…" He scrapes a hand across his face. He does not want to mention my mate's death. He knows it would be inappropriate and inconsiderate of my mourning. It may have been a hundred years, but among the Ssedez, often longer. The social stigma if I should mate before that would be a shadow over the new relationship. It would not be unusual for me to never mate again. The strength of our biological Attachment for our lover is that severe. In the case of a normal Attachment that lasts a lifetime, such strong bonds are a precious, invaluable miracle. But in the case of a death, it is unspeakably tragic.

For Oten, who has never been Attached, to form the Attachment for a human is one thing, but for me, one who lost a mate to humans…it is an indescribably painful catastrophe. Pvotton understands this.

"It is my problem," I say tightly. "I will handle it."

"But Gahnin, please let us help you. This is above and beyond any obligation to—"

"She is my duty!" I shout, and I cringe at the assertion in my voice. It sounds too much like the authority of a male in the throes of the Attachment. I am out of control; I am at my body's hormonal mercy. But there is a safety net for me. "I may have formed a physical Attachment, but the other biological stages—the heart's emotional bond, the soul-deep merging, the willingness to sacrifice my life for hers—will not occur. For gods' sakes, I could never bite her! And she will never, under any star in the heavens, return it. She hates me."

He heaves a deep sigh of relief. "True, true."

I add for my certainty as well as his, "I will be unable to form a true Attachment to her. There is no danger."

His expression changes to light optimism. "Perhaps it

is best for you to service her. Satisfy the physical bond and experience the rejection of the rest of the stages. It could be the best way. It should work."

"It will." I try hard to steady my breathing that I did not realize had quickened. "It has to."

He nods in confirmation. "If you change your mind, my offer is not rescinded. I will check on you again in the morning."

"Thank you."

He leaves, and I feel a sense of relief. This physical Attachment will die after I have satisfied the *desidre*. I may as well indulge in it.

But a forgotten truth slides into my gut. There is a piece Pvotton did not think of.

I have not been inside a female since Tiortan. We were mated so young, I have never been inside another female *but* her. It is unusual, though not unheard of, for the Attachment to form with one's first lover, but once it does, the desire to experiment with any other dies.

I have been without a female for a century. It's never bothered me until I met Assura. Now, my body's urgency is making her even more irresistible. It should not, but I am too far gone with the combination of the *desidre* and the Attachment to think otherwise.

I turn to look at her again, at the exquisitely formed body encased in the suit they put on her. Her formidable strength arouses me. When she attacked me, rather than stopping her, or negotiating with her, I wanted her to fight me. I liked it. It turned me on to watch her, feel her assert her strength.

She lies on her back, and even in her dreams, the *desidre* is tormenting her. Her nipples are rounded hard and outlined. Her head tosses, and those erotic sounds I have become so familiar with whimper in her throat.

In twelve hours, the new dose of *topuy* the medic gave us

this morning will wear off, and we will become animals to the *desidre*. Sex will be unavoidable, as we'll be that desperate to quench the fire.

I let go of my horror at her being human—I will remember that tomorrow—and free the fantasies that have been beckoning me since last night, since I slid my fingers into her slick, swollen, luscious cunt. I fantasize what it would be like to free my cock and watch it disappear into the depths of her, to feel her wetness swallow me, and to take her body with the desire raging within me.

What I would do to her...

Allowing my imagination to wander, I plan what I will do, how I will excite her, arouse her, and make her come. How I will use her and pound her body full of as much of me as she can take. How I will love hearing her scream and beg for more.

The rage of desire flooding me is beyond any torture or pleasure I have felt—perhaps ever. The chemical-induced lust the *desidre* fills me with, combined with the physical Attachment I am experiencing, is lethal to my reason and reduces me to only the carnal need to mate. Which, in this moment, I no longer have to fight.

I'm aware of every piece of myself. Blood courses through my veins, heated and thick. I am hard and can think of nothing but spreading her legs and tasting her.

Darkness falls, and the light in the room fades. I can see only the outline of her body. And hear her.

She moans in her sleep and murmurs, "Gahnin..." She is dreaming about me.

My cock knows it, too. It swells, demanding to be within her, to give her what her voice tells me she needs. What I feel radiating off her like a live pulse on the air.

Her breathing becomes ragged, and her hands begin to move over her body. First her breasts and her middle, then gliding down between her legs. She locates the zipper in her suit and slides it down.

To see her finding pleasure in herself turns me on as much as the sound of her saying my name. I am torn between the desire to touch her and the need to watch her.

She slides her hands inside the suit, between her thighs, and cries out the same sound she made yesterday when I touched her there. She must have found the spot that brings her so much pleasure.

Her back arches off the bed. And she wakes.

She stills, and her head turns to me.

I cannot see her face in the darkness, but I can feel her stare on me. I move forward but force myself not to go to her without invitation. "Assura?"

Her breath shudders, and she groans in frustration, pulls her limbs from her suit, and tosses it to the floor. "I need you to touch me."

I am beside her on her bed, my hands aching to be on her. I reach forward to caress the mound of her breasts, and she grips my forearms, encouraging me.

"More," she begs.

Through force of will, I retract my fangs. It is agony, them pushing back inside my gums, and the buildup of the venom will be excruciating when this is over, but what I want more than to bite her is…

To kiss her. Everywhere.

Chapter Five

Assura

His lips meet mine, and…and…I never knew.

What it felt like to be kissed like he'll die if he can't. To be kissed like his life and breath depend on my returning that kiss. Like the world could disintegrate, and he wouldn't know it—that's how much he needs to kiss me.

My lips are helpless not to follow. I'm unable not to respond.

In the darkness, the reasons to not do this don't matter. That he is the last person I should ever touch this way, that for me to take pleasure in a Ssedez is a criminal irony in conjunction with my past is insignificant. There is only him, and my lust for his body, and his desire for mine.

The softness of his lips combines with the hardness of his claiming. My mouth belongs to him, his mouth tells me, and I revel in the fierce pull of his sucking lips over mine. At the forceful thrust of his tongue into my mouth and…

My gods.

His tongue—the length of it, the dexterity of it.

The long twin tips wrap around my tongue in a spiral—and massage mine. I never knew a tongue could be massaged, but he does. He squeezes it from the back to the tip. It pulls the tension from my throat and lengthens my tongue, until it's between his lips and in his mouth.

He frees it, untangles his tongue from mine, and moans as I return the caresses. I push my tongue as deep into his mouth as it will go, him sucking it deeper with his lips, coaxing me to explore him.

The press of his mouth against mine…it's like he's delving inside of me, pulling me into him and begging to feel me want him.

And I do, sweet gods, how I do.

I grab his shoulders and grip his neck, pulling his mouth even harder against my own. How he wants me… I want more. I need more.

The need to feed off him, his body and his desire, is like a force of nature inside me. There is no logic or train of thought or resistance. It's all gone.

There is only him.

His mouth travels to my throat, and his lips and tongue stroke over the sensitive, vulnerable hollow there. He is thorough, as though needing to taste every inch of my skin.

But I am impatient. The hunger from my very center—the clenching from deep within me starving to be filled by him—there is no stopping it or calming it.

I grab at his waist, his back, pulling him against me.

His breath not leaving my skin, he pushes his leathers off, then climbs over me, naked.

I open my legs for him, so impatient to have him in me, pounding me, I have no need for more foreplay.

But he disagrees. He kneels between my legs but does not rest on top of me.

The tip of his distended cock drags across my belly, but when I reach for it, he pulls away and kisses down my chest. He grasps my breasts, and just the feel of his palms over my achingly hard nipples has me writhing. The tickle of his skin is a torture worse than any mouth or tongue—even his.

"Please, Gahnin. I—need—" I seethe in agony, the need to orgasm like a storm racing through my body, threatening to burst with lightning at any moment.

He caresses my cheek and whispers in my ear, "I will take care of you."

The certainty of his words, it's almost a threat...or...a vow. Something that rings like far more than a commitment to make me come.

He drags his hands down my waist, his mouth hovering over my belly as though he regrets not giving it more attention. But then, to my relief, his head drifts between my legs.

It may not be his cock, but it's the next best thing.

He kisses my clit first, with just his lips, and sucks.

I arch my hips toward his mouth and am helpless not to grasp his head. I tangle my hands in his hair and beg for him to give me more.

Then he uses his tongue, the long flesh circling my clit in one flick, and he spins it.

"Ah, ah, ah..." I cannot contain my sounds. I don't know how this pleasure is possible, but I am so close to bursting in climax, the demand aches like a bomb fuse burning up my spine.

He lowers his mouth, presses his thumb to my clit, massaging it with delectable pressure. His tongue strokes through my folds then licks inside me—deeper and deeper—until he's reaching and licking as far into me as I go.

It's too much—my whole body too desperate to climax—the pleasure he's filling me with too much to bear.

I come, pumping my hips. Tension seizes me, and I am

immobile as the excruciating ecstasy washes through me—covering me and consuming me.

But it is not enough.

The orgasm has barely finished me, and I'm reaching for his shoulders. "Your—cock—now."

I'm still empty. Aching for a need to have him filling me and coming in me.

He sits up on his knees, the shadow of his massive body outlined in the glow from the hallway. He grasps my waist and pulls my thighs up onto his lap, widening my hips around his.

There's a delicious stretch through my abdomen, his thighs supporting my lower back, and a satisfying opening between my legs. He brushes against my sensitive wet folds, and a shudder rolls through his limbs.

His hands shake as they grip my outer thighs, and the raggedness of his breathing has me a little worried for him.

He notches his hard tip into me and freezes; even his breathing stops.

I ache, reaching for his hands, wanting him to thrust into me in one hard drive. "Gahnin!"

His breathing restarts, somehow both even and ragged at the same time. Then he does exactly as I hoped with a jerk of my hips onto his.

And thrusts full into me.

"AH!" I clench around him. The stretching. The exquisite size of him. I am filled. Wide and deep, he touches everywhere inside me that can be touched.

The harsh groan he makes sounds from so far within him, it's as though he wants this even more than I do. Which I can't imagine is possible.

I hook my ankles around his back, pulling him as far into me as he can go. Though he's already there.

He presses his thumb to my clit again and continues his

perfect circles. He rocks his hips into me, thrusting, rubbing me inside as he rubs me outside. It lights me up, my whole body climaxing without warning. I'm gripping him in a fierce pulse with keening, brutal cries.

He answers me, driving into me harder, faster, making the orgasm seem to go on. I feed on him.

He feeds me.

The urgency of his thrusts slides the mattress across the floor, as though the very earth beneath me quakes with his carnal lust to have me.

Then he starts to come.

And it's violent.

His body trembles. Any restraint disappears. His grip on both my hips so hard, it bruises me deliciously. I need his desperation as much as I crave his come.

The growl that tears from him is like something from his soul, from the very root of the animal he is, and he climaxes inside me.

I gasp, feeling his fluid flow within me.

It soaks me, a flood of his virility so strong, it fills me wholly until it pours out of me. And he keeps going. His come slickens me, so he speeds his thrusts, jerking me against him in a pounding faster and faster until I'm orgasming from the sheer force of him quaking into my body.

He slows, but the weight of his grip on me does not lessen. The shudder of his body speeds to an almost shiver, and his voice sounds harsh and desperate. "Can I—give you—more?"

The stun in me—that after that he can do more—I search myself. He's drenching my thighs, his pounding spreading his come all over my skin. It's not enough, though. I do want more. Forever and ever more.

"Y-y-yes." I hiss, incapable of more than a whisper.

He groans, a deep rumble of a sound, one of territorial need. He flips me onto my knees, pulls my ass into the air, his fingers squeezing my hips back against his.

And surges inside me again.

I keen with gratitude and, free to move in this pose, I rise onto my arms and meet his drives with all the force of every muscle in my body.

I lose myself to him, my mind fading and drifting away with the tide of sex—with him.

He becomes everything. Him and his cock.

I am made for this. This is how it should always be. Him fucking me. Me taking it and loving it.

He does it again and again, until we're both so wasted with exhaustion and spent with erotic sensation, we can no longer move.

And we sleep.

Chapter Six

GAHNIN

I did not mean for it to happen. Or I did, but I did not know how thick the dam was inside me and how much it was holding back. Now I have let it out…

It is not enough. It feels as though it will never be enough. As though fucking her once only made me want more.

The sensation of unquenchable need is so similar to the Attachment mating frenzy, I lie awake, unable to sleep, the dread and confusion beating through my blood, scourging everything I thought I knew about myself.

All that sex did not help. Pvotton was wrong. I was wrong. The beginning of the Attachment is not abated. It is not satisfiable. My fangs seem perma-extended, my cock no less so, and the only thing keeping me from reaching for her again is her need for sleep.

She is not Ssedez. She is not built genetically for the Attachment-related mating frenzy as a female Ssedez would be. Assura is still healing. Hopefully, feeding her *desidre* so well will help.

Oh gods. I dig my fingers in my hair and stand, getting away from her. I do not care about her healing. I have no concern for her well-being. It matters to me only that she is well enough to travel to the human crash site.

That is the only reason I care. It is not because she means anything to me emotionally. I care nothing for her. It's impossible. My heart is rioting, screaming that I feel something for her, but it is a cruel, cruel liar. It wants me to look back at her, to stare at her naked body, to listen to her breathe. It wants me to not leave her side.

Unthinkable.

I pace. It is the only option. I stare out the glass wall into the hall, standing vigil for when someone, anyone, will come to us with the dawn. Our dosage of *topuy* has not yet worn off. This sexcapade was caused only by the natural need to feed the beginnings of *desidre*. The fever, the pain-inducing fire, has not even overtaken us yet. It is going to get worse.

I breathe a silent yell, huffing through my clenched teeth. I would make a sound loud enough to wake the whole town, but I do not want to wake her. I do not want to speak to her. I do not want to see her eyes when she looks at me.

I regret bitterly not taking Pvotton up on his offer of removing me from this cell. The sex was too good, Assura too much of what I craved, too perfectly suited to meeting my every sexual need and feeding my every desire, stoking it hotter than it already was. Her passion is a force I want to experience again, while bringing her to such pleasure, she can think of mating with no other than me.

My fangs throb in my gums with agony. Their sweet, syrupy venom pools inside my mouth, intended for bonding her with ecstasy to me. This is not happening.

This is not happening!

This. Is. Not. Happening.

Too many hours of waiting, of begging the sun to rise, of desperation for someone, anyone, to come so I can get away from her.

But as the first rays of dawn trickle through the windows, before anyone else appears, she wakes. Her eyes open on me, hazy at first, and then there's a flash of memory, of the pleasure from last night, along with a longing for more.

She looks around the cell, at where we are, and recognition widens her eyes. Her gaze wanders back to me, and bitter revulsion curls her lip, as though, if she could, she would run from the room to get away from me.

Her hatred of me is undiminished. I share the sentiment. She grabs her suit, which I folded next to her, and clothes herself.

I resume my pacing, determined to avoid staring at her.

"Did they give us the *topuy* or something?" she mutters. "I don't feel the *desidre* fever."

"We are still on yesterday's dose."

She scoffs. "Great. Something to look forward to."

"Koviye said the punishment is for only a day. It may get unbearable for a few hours at the end, but then it will be over."

"An hour is too long," she snaps. "You haven't experienced the hell of it." I glance at her and shouldn't. I catch her staring at my groin.

There is only one comfort, which is not a comfort at all: she still wants me.

Must not think about it. "I remember how you were when you came in from the jungle. I have no desire to experience that."

She leans her head back against the wall. "Which means either more marathon sex with you to fend off the *desidre*, or more of the worst pain imaginable. Neither option is attractive."

Something in me snaps. It is part of the Attachment, the

possessive part, the drive to keep her for myself and ensure no other male will touch her.

She is lying. But she needs to know it.

"The sex was so terrible?" I mock, knowing it's not true. She loved every minute. She was so hungry for more of me, the only reason she stopped was because of fatigue.

She avoids looking at me and stares at the ceiling. "It was so bad, I can't even talk about it." But as I watch, her nipples pebble beneath the tight material covering her chest, and she stretches her legs in front of her—her thighs rubbing together in discomfort.

I should not care. Her comfort, her desire, is no business of mine. The only business I should be in right now is getting away from her. But as much as I loathe myself for it, the need to make sure she desires me, and only me, is a physiological imperative.

I sit back against the wall. She may be two meters across the cell, but I can smell her arousal. "It was so bad, you crave more." This is not a question. I know it is true.

She tightens her fists and does not answer.

I want to hear her say it. "You want it. To be the sex-crazed animal you were with me. But it scares you."

"Shut up," she snaps through her teeth.

"You liked it—how badly I wanted you. How much I could not get enough of you, and how I made you come again and again." How badly I still want to. How much I shouldn't. But how much it makes me want to torture her even more.

She whimpers and pinches her lips together, but her legs open, almost like she wants me to look.

I do. I know what it feels like now—between her thighs. "Your cunt is so sweet. Hot and slick. Perfect for sex. Lots of it. Hard and rough." My breath is speeding, wanting it, wanting her. Her eyes close and her lips part, like she's imagining it. "Gods, sinking my cock in you—fucking you while you tighten around me like a fist every time I make you come. I could do it all day. And I will, when the antidote wears off. If you can take it."

Her hand slips between her legs, and I watch her rub herself where she aches.

I lower my voice, speaking as much to myself now as her. "You know you should not. But it does not stop you from wanting me."

"Yes," she whispers without looking at me.

"It is only because of the *desidre*." Saying it has me rethinking my obsession with getting away from her. "It is the only thing that could get us to fuck again."

Her hand stills, and she meets my eyes. She knows I'm right.

I sneer, not hiding my revulsion. "I hate you. You hate me. Sex between us is only about necessity." But I let free my guttural need to be inside her again and growl, "We can agree that beyond feeding the *desidre,* this goes nowhere."

She nods, and some tension leaves her shoulders. "Agreed." Her gaze drops to my cock again, visibly erect under my leather uniform, and she licks her lips.

The door to the cell clicks open, but no one is there, as though it opened by itself. Then, as though it's a trick of the light, a being forms, glowing at first, then solidifying until Koviye stands in front of us.

Assura and I stare at him. She asks before I can, "You can disappear?"

Koviye smirks, "It is a talent of mine, yes." What skin is visible outside of his iridescent robe—his hands, his neck and face—loses its glowing light and subsides into undulating shades of blue. I look closer, and the changing blues are almost like a manifestation of energy or something of the sort.

He is not of brute stature like the Ssedez warriors, but he

is far from weak. There is a dominance about him that makes me think his near-constant smile is merely a distraction. I would not want to be his enemy.

He spreads his arms and says with roguish mischief, "I'm brilliant. In case you didn't already know."

"Congratulations. I'm thrilled for you," Assura says dryly.

"Cling to your scasms—carmsim, scarsim, oh what's the word?" He hums a moment. "Learning a language in a week has its negatives."

"Do you mean 'sarcasm'?" Assura supplies.

"Ah, yes." Koviye gives her a conciliatory nod. "That is the word. Regardless of your attitude, you are the one benefitting from my success in this case. I will accept your thanks later. Although—" He looks at us more closely. "Oh, good for you! Just as I suspected. This may be sad news then."

I scowl at his lack of clarity. "What are you talking about?"

He steps toward me, seeming to examine my skin. "At least three times, yes? Or four? Definitely less than six." He turns to Assura. "And you are glowing with good health in comparison to yesterday. Am I right in guessing six, more?" He glances back at me as though for confirmation. "Job well done."

"Six what?" Assura snaps. She may have lost count as the time passed, but I know what he's referring to. I kept track. The correct number of climaxes she experienced is eight.

"Orgasms, dear," Koviye answers. "Your blood runs clean. You have fed the *desidre* and are sufficiently satisfied, for the time being."

"You can tell?" she gasps. "You can see my blood?"

"Naturally. All the Fellamana can. Nemona and Oten tell me it is a unique gift of our species. Such a pity for you."

"Koviye." I scratch my head, willing myself to have

patience. "You brought news, you said. What have you accomplished?"

He gives a heavy, fake sigh. "I'm afraid it won't be good news for you anymore."

"We can decide that for ourselves, thanks," Assura snaps.

He leans his shoulder against the wall, which could be casual, except he seems hungry for our reactions, almost bloodthirsty. "Yours truly," he points at himself, proudly, "convinced the elders that your little fight in the hospital was a form of foreplay and not violence with intent of physical harm." He clears his throat and gives us both skeptical looks.

Assura and I glance at each other, our eyes locking. We are free. We can leave this cell, and I will never have to touch her or be in the same room with her again. She is healed. We can continue on with our mission to locate her crew, if she will do it without fighting me this time.

Koviye adds, "You are freed from imprisonment. You will continue to receive the *topuy* and will not be subjected to the full force of the *desidre*."

I should be filled with relief, but my chest concaves, making it difficult to breathe. I feel...loss. Which I do not understand. The only thing I am losing is forced proximity to this human. I will rejoice to no longer have to be alone with her. I refuse to experience disappointment at not having to have intimate contact with her.

It is merely the sex, the touch of a female. I will, after this, have to pursue other Ssedez females. That is all this feeling signifies. But that thought twists my stomach as though with a sickness.

I search for a response in Assura, but her expression is a cold stare, vacant of emotion. I can only assume she is concealing her elation at our separation.

"Do I sense disappointment?" Koviye asks in provocation.

"No," Assura and I snap simultaneously.

Koviye's face cracks, and he guffaws with laughter. "Oh dear, this is a tragedy. Why do you deny it? I fail to understand the logic of your species. Desire should be freely expressed. There is no shame in it."

Anger at him swells in my chest, and I have to clench my fists to push him from blocking our exit. "Let us out," I say with crisp authority.

He composes himself. "You could at least say thank you."

Assura and I both coolly say the words by force, and I move around him toward the door. I need out of this cell and away from *her*. There is work to be done. I must clear my head of this lustful distraction and return to duty.

"Not so fast." Koviye halts my exit. "There is one condition."

Assura asks before I can, "What did you do, Koviye?"

I glance back at him, and his complexion deepens from its rainbow hues of blue to a deep navy. "They want a demonstration."

"Of what?" I growl.

"Your exquisite sexual attraction. It's practically oozing off you. Phew!" He wipes his brow as though overheated. "You two are steaming with it."

"What kind of demonstration?" Assura pushes.

"How to translate it? That's the difficult part." Koviye taps his chin, keeping us deliberately in suspense.

"Say it!" I snap.

"You can choose to stay here and serve out your full punishment. Or, in exchange for your early freedom, before the worst of the *desidre* overcomes you, you are to participate in tonight's Sex Games."

Chapter Seven

Assura

"No, absolutely, no," I protest at the same time Gahnin says, "Impossible. We cannot."

Koviye makes a ticking noise with his tongue as if scolding us. "Would you rather be subjected to the *desidre* fever with no *topuy*?"

I shiver in revulsion, and I have no response. Whatever these "Sex Games" are, it can't be worse.

Koviye lifts his brows. "Besides, you will once again be given the excuse to pleasure each other, which apparently you are incapable of doing without outside motivation." He rolls his eyes.

"But what do we have to do?" Gahnin asks.

"If you can't guess, I'll leave it a mystery." He drops his lighthearted tone and adds seriously, "Your participation would help you gain favor with my people. The Fellamana believe how people make love shows who they truly are. There is no better way to earn their trust for both your species than to show them how you mate." Koviye walks from the cell.

We're given no further explanation, and two other Fellamana enter. "Do you consent to be contestants in the Sex Games?" one says with a singsonging accent.

I glance at Gahnin, and his expression is veiled. I can't tell if he's enthused or not. His tone is as neutral as his expression. "We are compatible physically and—"

I spit with laughter. "Compatible? Understatement of the universe."

He scowls. "And if it will help with diplomacy, I am willing. The choice ultimately, though, is yours." His attempt to not give away his excitement fails. I recognize the way his hands flex—he's thinking about touching me again and wants it. Good thing I want it, too. Good thing I'm game for any adventure that involves him.

"All right, in the name of diplomacy." I face the Fellamana. "We consent." I can't say it with a straight face. Never would I ever have thought diplomacy and sex could go together, but however these games are going to work, I'm into the surprise of finding out.

They separate Gahnin and me. We're each taken out and led in opposite directions.

From the name, I have a pretty good idea that these games involve having sex in public, with some sort of competitive aspect to it. The conflict in me rages with uncertainty. I'm glad to be rid of Gahnin. I need space, and getting away from him is a good thing. It should be. Except my body wants him back. I didn't realize that when we agreed to have sex through the *desidre* fever, I'd begun to look forward to being with him.

I can still feel the stretch between my legs where he was inside me, over and over. Gods, the craving is not gone. How is that possible? I've never had so much sex at one time in my life. I've never wanted to so much. I've never wanted more like this. It's never felt so powerfully, soul-quenchingly good. I can't blame myself for wanting more. This *desidre,* even while not at full force, sure as hell makes it good.

I have to find someone else to satisfy the *desidre* with. I can't keep doing this with Gahnin. My emotions think it's about needing more of *him* alone. It's confusing. It's just the *desidre.*

"These Sex Games," I ask the Fellamana female accompanying me. "Do I have to be with Gahnin? Could I choose someone else?"

Her complexion is different from Koviye's shades of sapphire and navy. She's more a warm yellow, like sunlight, that blends into orange and every shade in between. Her skin changes when she speaks, almost like it's linked to her emotions or her words.

There's a look of confusion on her face, and she says something to me in her musical language that I can't understand. *Damn.* Lost in translation.

"Can I speak to Koviye?" I ask.

"Koviye?" she repeats.

"Yes."

She says something ending in a downward tone that even in a foreign language sounds like a negative. I give up my attempts at communication.

I'm frustrated we are again delayed in getting to my fellow rebels. I should be there helping them. I have to find them. I have to get to them to do everything I can. I need to prove to them all and myself that I am capable of saving people, not just hurting them, not just killing them. I have to get back to that work, to leave behind this existence that seems defined by having sex, again and again. As much as I'm enjoying it.

Gahnin. I feel guilt. I am guilty.

I shouldn't be sharing anything with him, let alone something so intimate and ecstatic. If he knew what I'd done while a Ten Systems special operative under General Dargule's command and threats, I'd be dead.

When I escaped from under Dargule's thumb with the *Origin* and its crew, I tried to sneak his prisoners, including one long-held Ssedez, off his ship. I did try, I swear. But things didn't go according to plan. In the end, I had to choose: either save the rebellion and ensure the *Origin's* safe escape, or save the prisoners. I made my choice.

That is why, with Gahnin, these sexual experiences, him giving me orgasms and me receiving the pleasure—the irony of it makes my heart ache. I shouldn't accept it. I should confess to Gahnin what I've done and repel him, then the desire I see in his eyes every time he looks at me would die.

But I'm a coward. I can't tell him. I don't want to tell him. I want to leave it in the past, to move forward with my new life and not have to wallow in the guilt of it all.

I will make it right with the Ssedez. Somehow. I don't know how. But I will fix it.

The Fellamana female, whose name I learn is Dalinya, grooms me and bathes me. It's nice and comforting, even with her thoroughness. She gives me a selection of clothes to choose from. I do as she instructs.

My mind is elsewhere.

Gahnin and I are joined now in this Sex Games debacle, and it's my fault. When I fought against him, I caused this problem. I should have cooperated. I should have trusted him, if for no other reason than it is my duty to make amends for what I did to his people. The wound I sustained in my side from one of his warriors in the battle... Now that I have full strength, now that my logic is back and it's not consumed with the *desidre,* I see this injury for what it truly is. It's an eye for an eye. Equal repayment.

I'll ask Koviye to let me fulfill my punishment in the games with a willing Fellamana. I can resist Gahnin now that the *desidre* in me is temporarily satisfied. Tomorrow, when Gahnin and his warriors leave for the *Origin's* crash site, I'll go with them without a fight. I'll do everything I can to try to build a bridge between our species, to ensure they are treated fairly by us in the rebellion. I have to follow General Nem's orders.

Satisfied with my conclusion, I pay more attention to the Fellamana dress I've put on and can't hide a laugh. To call the Fellamana sexually adventurous is putting it mildly. They're not just free-loving, they're…quite prurient.

Downright sexualized. With zero shame.

Dalinya coos at my dress. It's a willowy, sleeveless robe. It flows to my ankles in iridescent fabric. It's stunning, and I'm about to smile and say thank you when I realize the cutouts are in all the wrong places. Or the *right* places, I guess.

The neckline isn't a neckline. It's a square cut below my breasts, forcing them to peek out over the top. There's a slit up the middle that I assume is for my legs, until I realize it goes up to my navel. My crotch is exposed with every step I take.

I am on display.

Dalinya is enamored with my pubic area, like having curls there is some sort of commodity. When I put together that the Fellamana and the Ssedez don't have body hair, her fascination makes me feel like a sex goddess.

Gahnin seemed fascinated, too. Though my impatience for him to do other things to me made me rush him in his curiosity.

Dalinya is so kind, even in her liberal attentions to my backside, where she makes the cutout over my ass even higher. She implies my muscled posterior is something she likes, though I don't know for sure, with our massive language barrier.

It makes me miss talking to Jenie, my friend, sometimes

lover, among the rebels on the *Origin*. I wonder if she's still alive.

I focus on the female in front of me, and for fun, let Dalinya squeeze my ass so she can assess what it feels like and lift one of my legs to see what my curls cover up. Heat lines her eyes as she looks at me and touches me, and I'm happy to learn the Fellamana are not strictly heterosexual. Though I'm not surprised, as free-loving as they are.

It would be normal for me to ask her if she'd like to indulge in a little pleasurable pregame. But I am distracted.

I'm desperate to ask her more questions—what's coming? What happens at the Sex Games? But that Koviye didn't teach either of us more in the other's language makes me think the barrier is intentional.

They don't want me to know; it's part of the game and the punishment.

Luckily, Dalinya seems to understand without insult that my desires are elsewhere at the moment. She gives me a delicate kiss on the lips and whispers something in her language that sounds like a combination of good luck, well-wishes, and blessings.

I stroke her cheek. "Thank you."

I gesture to my bare feet and ask for shoes.

She shakes her head with a smile and leads me out the door barefoot, escorting me from the changing area through an underground tunnel. When we resurface from underground, I'm added to a line of a half dozen Fellamana dressed like me. Their robes expose all private parts, too. They're competitors, it seems like.

I wish I could talk to them. I smile and wave hello. They bow in greeting.

We stand in the entranceway to an arena, where I guess the games will take place. The participants lift their chins high in pride. It's obviously a huge honor to be chosen for the games. Spectators of Fellamana walk past us, gazing their fill.

They're appreciative with compliments but not creepy with sexualized taunts. Not like humans do sometimes. It's as though our bodies are paintings in a museum. They fawn over me but give greetings in their language and smile, too.

I might actually like being looked at. After decades being in the military, forced to wear formless armor daily that hid my gender, it's freeing to be seen as female—except I'm too busy looking for Koviye and trying to think of a way I could convince him that my punishment could still be acted out with someone other than Gahnin.

Also, I'm trying to distract myself from hoping he says no and that I'll have to be with Gahnin anyway. Luckily, Gahnin has not appeared, so I haven't had to see how they dressed him. Gods, if they have his glorious cock on display, my resolve to resist him will probably go to hell.

"Assura!" Koviye comes forward with arms wide. "The Sex Games dress suits you." His gaze roams over my body and meets my eyes with warmth. "I predict you will be the highlight of the evening." For the first time, he seems genuine. The expression of restrained laughter he's had each time I've met him is gone. Instead, he has an easy smile.

Koviye leans toward me. "I am anxious to witness the sexual prowess of this Ssedez who has such an effect on you. I need to know his skills."

"Are you in need of pointers?" I jibe.

"There's never such a thing as too many pleasure skills, and I know many. But I don't know the ways a human woman would be pleased." His face turns from cerulean to a light sky blue, as though his emotions lightened with the color change.

"What good will human ways do you?"

"There is a woman among your human crew who I would learn how to court in your culture. She is—how do you say it—uptight?" He whispers it, as though this is something inexplicably sexy.

"You met the crew? Were you at the crash site?"

"For a week, I observed them to be sure they were no danger to the Fellamana."

I frown. "Sounds like you were stalking them, and one in particular."

"Would you rather I waged war against them for being uninvited strangers like the Ten Systems would?" He shudders like I've insulted him. "Spying is preferable to violence, and I spent a lot of time witnessing the work of your acting general taking Nemona's place while she is gone with her Ssedez. Jenie is her name."

My heart skips, and it's my turn to grab Koviye by the shoulders. "Jenie is alive?"

"You know her?"

I can't help it. I wrap my arms around him and hug him. Tears brim in my eyes, and I murmur, "Praise and thanks to every god there is." The greatest relief I've felt since landing here rushes through my chest. I'll get to see her again. Tomorrow. I have to get to my dearest friend tomorrow.

But around us, the arena is filling, and the games could start anytime. I almost forgot. "Koviye, I'd like to have a Fellamana for a partner in the Sex Games instead of Gahnin."

His brow furrows as if I've said something incomprehensible. "But why? You burn for him. I saw it in you this afternoon. There is no reason—"

"My reasons are my own, thank you very much. I don't want him." The lie trips on my tongue, and I have to swallow and cool my expression to hide it.

"You don't…want him?" His mouth opens and closes as if not knowing what to say. "Is my translation off? I must not be understanding you correctly."

I inhale for patience. "No, you understand. I want someone else."

"We certainly would not force you. Consent is as sacred as nonviolence among the Fellamana." He steps closer, his lips pressing together with concern. "I will find you someone else, if you're sure."

"Did you say, 'someone else'?" Gahnin's voice comes thick and ominous behind me.

I turn and...words fail me.

Leather straps, that's all Gahnin wears. They crisscross his massive chest, making his abs and pecs look impossibly harder than they already are. They wrap the top of his hips then circle around his back, doing I can only imagine what to show off his ass, then circle around his thighs and twine down his legs. His quads bulging and flexing...

But none of that matters, because of what's in the middle. The lengths of leather draw the eye to his most spectacular asset.

I knew he was big but—my, oh my. He's even more stunning than I remembered.

His cock is perfection. An impressive length as well as girth. Obscene but not grotesque. As though the Ssedez female anatomy he's made for must be similar to that of the human female.

He hangs, or almost hangs because he's protruding outward as well, to his mid-thigh. He's partially erect, thick and swelling. And there are adornments—a golden piece of jewelry that attaches to the base of his cock and hangs on a small chain downward. It emphasizes his size—not that he needs it, but this is the Fellamana who are dressing him.

But the thing that most intrigues me is the flaring crown of the jewel. It protrudes above his cock flat against his pelvis, and I can only imagine what it would feel like while he pounded inside me, to feel it rubbing against my clit...

He clears his throat. I'm blatantly staring. Which was the Fellamana's point in his garb, but I finally tear my eyes upward and glance at his face.

His eyes burn, like the hottest of blue flames. He glares at me with such sexual demand, I'm surprised I'm not already on my back with my legs spread for him. I would—if there weren't so many people around.

I was right. One look at him, and my will to resist him has crumbled.

"There will be no one else," he growls, his words rumbling in his chest and sending unexpected tremors of arousal from my head to my toes. His fangs protrude from his mouth, descending past his lower lip at my eye level.

Fascinated, I reach to feel them.

He grasps my wrist before I can. "Do not touch."

Koviye chuckles behind us and severs our locked gaze. "Assura, I'm guessing you have changed your mind?"

Gahnin interrupts me from answering. "It is either sex with me or no sex at all."

I gape at him. "Are you serious?" Where did this male-must-claim-female shit come from? And what's more confusing...why do I kind of...like it? Even in my outrage, it's causing heat to gather in my center. Thinking of fucking anyone but him is a non-option anyway right now. But still.

He nudges my elbow and turns us away from Koviye so we can talk without being overheard. "Why would you have need for someone else? Do I not satisfy you?" There is grit in his tone. He knows he satisfies me plenty; he's daring me to tell him otherwise.

But I'm not giving in to him that easily. "Maybe I want someone different. Maybe I've had enough of you."

He bares his fangs, and an animallike hiss issues from his mouth. "You think you have experienced all of me in one night?"

I stare at his fangs and know what I want. "Would you bite me this time?" I can't explain why I want it. Getting bitten should hurt, but the way they come out only when he's hard, the way he looks at me with scorching heat whenever they're extended, makes me think his fangs would have an erotic effect on me that I would like as much as his cock.

He jerks back from me as though I have slapped him. "Never."

I hold my hands up in surrender. "Okay, okay, fine. No biting." I can't deny the sliver of disappointment that seeps into my stomach.

He closes his eyes and takes a deep breath as though trying to calm himself. "Look, I know you hate me because my warriors brought down your ship and attempted to kill you."

My breath quickens. That is the opposite of what he's supposed to think. Now is my moment. Here is where I confess to him what I have done in my past life with the Ten Systems so that he refuses me. So that his urge to have sex with me changes to a desire to kill me.

He mistakes my hesitation. "For diplomacy's sake, we need to make this right with the Fellamana. I promise to make it good for you. Better than last night."

But my throat clenches. Maybe I can make this right another way, because I want him and he wants me and Koviye is right, why deny ourselves the indulgence? Why should I deny Gahnin what he wants?

"You're right," I say. "Let's find out the rules of this sex game."

I have to find out if my new plans for giving Gahnin the pleasure of his life fall within the parameters of the game.

Chapter Eight

Gahnin

Koviye explains the rules of the game: points for most adventurous, points for number of orgasms. He separates us, and I am led by a Fellamana to the opposite side of the arena from Assura. Like we are on an opposing team.

I sit on a glass bench, with Assura in full view across the stage from me. She is exposed and exquisite. I am unable to control my physical reactions to her. Her tight breasts perch outside her robe. Her navel and the treasure trove between her thighs are visible to everyone.

They're all watching her.

The pull to cross the arena to get to her is fierce in my gut. There's a raised platform, a stage of sorts, between us. It is a bed the size of a match ring. I climb the steps, but someone grabs my arm. A Fellamana guard pulls me back, and I'm forced back to my bench.

I cover my face with my hands. It is as though I have become a slave to her—or a slave to my desire for her. The instinct in me to call her mine, to keep her and make sure no one else touches her, is getting stronger, not weaker.

When she asked me if I would bite her, a beast roared in my chest, crying *yes!* It is taking all of my willpower to suppress that voice. For me to get through this charade without biting her will be a miracle.

I do not know what is happening to me.

She is human. She is from the Ten Systems. Sharing my venom with her is an unthinkable possibility. My instinct, my carnal desire, is a traitor to my mind.

And my heart—it hurts.

Tiortan. My feelings are a betrayal to her in this hour.

All I swore on her death, all the vengeance I decreed I would bring her memory…it is slipping through my fingers like sand. Without my need for vengeance…I do not understand the world. My purpose has turned on its head, and I cannot tell which way is right and which way is wrong.

I cling to thoughts of tomorrow. My warriors and I will get out of this town and away from the Fellamana. To hell with the human; if she fights me again, I will leave her behind. I will tell Oten his assigned duty was impossible, and she was sabotaging our mission. If I want, I can never speak to her or look at her again. It will work. It has to. Or I will lose my sanity to her.

But I have to get through this. I have to fuck her again, first. And I promised I would make it better than before. I swear to every god, I do not know how I am going to live through this. I need a plan. Some survival strategy.

A melodious chime sounds through the arena. The Fellamana gasp with excitement and hurry to their seats that are made of—what else?—glass. A Fellamana dressed in an elaborate ceremonial robe stands in front of our line and speaks. Koviye appears at my side and gives me a wink.

I wish I could translate what the announcer is saying.

I do not even know the rules. "Explain this game to me, Koviye. What do the Fellamana consider adventurous?" If our participation is part diplomacy, I should know the expectations of the spectators.

"You will see. Your aggressive foreplay from the hospital the other day will be a requested starter."

A fight I can do.

There's a deafening roar from the crowd, and I realize thousands have filed into the seats shrouded in the dark above me. I cannot see beyond the bright lights highlighting the stage.

I make out the words "Ssedez" and "Ten Systems" from the announcer, and I am blinded by a spotlight. Koviye pushes me forward.

"Wave at them!" he calls over the deafening sound. "You want them to like you. That's the whole point of this."

I feign a smile and lift my hand.

Assura is in a similar spotlight across from me. At the sight of her, the ache in me to be inside her is intensely visceral. I'm torn between wanting to be next to her and wanting to be as far away as I can get.

"You are the stars of the show this evening," Koviye says.

"I thought this was a competition, not a show."

"I…" Koviye hesitates. "I don't think my translation is off. Perhaps it is both. Or maybe…a spectacle! That's the right word."

I clamp down on my impatience and grit, "I want to go first." To get it over with.

Koviye chuckles darkly. "Uh, no. You, our guests of honor, are last."

"How long is that?" I grumble.

"Hours."

I growl in protest and force myself to breathe deep. I have to get a hold over myself. I'm primed for her. My lack of control over myself is disturbing. I feel as though a feral beast has bred inside my chest, and the only meal it's starved for is her.

The Attachment.

The word seeps through my brain. I have to shake it out. What I feel starting is not real. It's a delusion. It has to be.

The emcee continues, and Koviye translates for me, detailing the intricate rules of the game that he described earlier. The points system for winning is more complex, but I disconnect after the fourth or fifth points category.

"The only number I care about," I mumble, "is the number of times she comes."

Koviye's shoulders shake with amusement. "That's how I play when I'm the main attraction."

"You've done this?"

"Many times. I have skills that, well…" He smirks like there's a private joke for him in this. "I'm a favorite, you might say. All Fellamana see the change in energy when either of you orgasms, so yes, the number of orgasms is the primary way of tallying points. Though there are extra for most original and creative. We like to be entertained."

He clears his throat to keep from laughing. "We love watching how different species make love. They saw Oten and Nemona but—"

"You saw Oten and Nemona?"

"Yes, they gave us a bit of a show. It makes us more excited to see you and Assura." He leans close to my ear. "They're dying to see your aggressive foreplay."

Which won't be difficult. I'm liable to tackle her the first chance I have, and she will no doubt want to fight first.

The contests begin, and it would be thrilling to watch, if I were not flooded with lust stealing my senses and robbing me of clear thought.

The Fellamana are creative. Much more creative than

I. Most acts—or scenes, as Koviye refers to them—are not merely couples but groups, varying in number and gender. Most are rather artistic. The crowd politely watches in silence and reserves their cheers for the end. Usually when the last male, if there is one, or more than one, climaxes.

I begin to have ideas, fantasies about what this setup will allow me to do to Assura, of the pleasurable things I could give her. There's an elaborate assortment of toys and devices spread on a table, which most participants make liberal use of. There's a grid of hanging apparatus above the bed, which they reset each time the whole stage and bed are cleaned between acts. Many enjoy using some suspension. Ideas keep mounting in my imagination, distracting me from how dishonorable it is for me to enjoy this whole scenario.

I wonder when the competition stops and if there's a time limit. I do not know how long I will keep going at Assura, but these paltry acts lasting less than thirty minutes are not comparable, if my need for her is anything like last night.

It feels worse.

I have begun to wonder if I will ever be flaccid again. It has yet to fully reduce in swelling today.

At the beginning of each scene, the participants go to two designated Fellamana who seem to be like referees. "What are they doing?" I ask Koviye.

"Setting hard limits. People can get carried away sometimes in the thrill of the crowd. Those two are there to interfere if anything goes beyond what another person is comfortable with."

Fear bursts in my chest, and I have to force myself to breathe. "I have to speak to Assura. I do not know what her limits are."

"You can't."

I face him and give him the full fury of my gaze. "I. Must. Speak. With. Her."

"It's against the rules."

"Damn the rules. I will storm this stage right now."

Koviye sighs heavily and puts hands on my shoulders. "Gahnin. Stay. The referees will tell you what she says before you begin. And you will be able to talk to her during your scene. That is the beauty and intimacy of the setup. You can speak, but we'll have no idea what you say."

This calms my immediate fury, but not my mounting anticipation.

Hours pass, scene after scene, until it is a monotony of bodies and sex. I witness sexual positions I never would have dreamed possible in groups of three or four. Polyamory is rare among the Ssedez. We are a serially monogamous people—a hazard with how we are genetically prone to the Attachment, but I wallow in the desire simmering through my veins, unable to focus on anything but getting to Assura.

It's torture.

The current scene, one of three males and one female, ends to thunderous cheers from the crowd.

"You're next," cries Koviye over the noise.

That fact does not bring me relief. It makes everything worse. My body aches.

The spotlights fall on me and Assura, and sweat sprouts on the back of my neck. With the way I feel right now, with my horror at myself for wanting her like I will stop breathing if I cannot have her, I barely register the Fellamana's announcement of our names. There is only her, and my fear of whether I can get through this and still know who I am when it's over.

We are led up the stage steps on opposite sides. We watch each other, and I am strangely comforted that her gaze is locked on me with a similar ferocity to mine.

She wants me.

Assura is taken to the referees first. She stands before

them like a goddess who has deigned to walk on two legs. The ends of her robe flow around her firm calves and thighs, tantalizing us, making us desperate for her to take it off.

That's the first thing I will do.

I suspect I'm not supposed to be able to hear her, but my Ssedez hearing is obviously more attuned than the Fellamana know.

Koviye translates the referees' questions for her. "How many partners are you comfortable having?"

I stiffen. I did not know adding someone else was an option. The feral animal in my chest roars in protest. It would beat the person bloody before it let someone else touch Assura.

I close my eyes and work for control. I can do this. I am not an animal. I am a sentient being with a rational mind. Breathe. Breathe.

I register Assura's, "Just Gahnin," and my eyes pop open in surprise.

Koviye translates again, his mouth stretched in a knowing smile. I wonder for a moment if he's saying all this just to torture us both. "Assura, you're sure you do not want a Fellamana to join you? Or another Ssedez? Gahnin's other warriors are watching."

I inhale to roar, *No!*

But I do not need to.

Assura shakes her head firmly and repeats, "Just Gahnin." It sends an irrational, misplaced sense of pride soaring through my limbs, but the referees begin to laugh.

"This may cost you the prestige of first place," Koviye says to her. "All the other scenes have had at least three and—"

Assura cracks a mischievous smile. "You have not seen us together yet."

It is like she has set fire to my veins, like I am a racer slamming on the gate at the starting line. I am done waiting.

It is time.

They ask her about more limits, and I listen like her word is my new sacred creed. She does not like pain. Bondage is fine, though she warns it never truly works on her because she can escape anything.

Interesting.

"Is there any point at which you'd like us to intervene?" Koviye asks.

Assura chuckles. "If it looks like I might kill him by accident, you're welcome to try to rescue him."

Koviye smiles, like he's humoring her and doesn't believe her. I know better. I know how formidable she is. Soon, the rest of them will know, too.

"Any questions for us?" Koviye asks.

She asks what I have been wondering. "Is there a time limit?"

"No," Koviye says. "It goes as long as he lasts."

It's Assura's turn for a humoring smile. "What if he can go for hours?"

Koviye pats her hand. "The pressure on a male of doing this in front of a crowd usually makes that impossible. So I wouldn't worry about it."

Assura glances at me with questioning brows raised.

I bow my head. *Challenge accepted.*

She bites her lip and walks to the center of the enormous bed on the dais, her feet dipping into the softness of the gigantic mattress. I cannot take my eyes off her. She is there. She is ready. The tilt to her walk, the swivel of her hip, she's taunting me.

The referees relay to me everything she said, and I already heard. They ask me my hard limits, of which I have none. They detail rules to me and how I must obey them, and if I try to give Assura anything she doesn't want, they'll stop me.

I hear them, but what I'm really watching is Assura.

She turns to me and slips her hand inside the robe, running her fingers up her inner thigh and licking her lips while she does it. She watches me, hard as stone and erect as steel, like she's thinking about tasting it.

That can be arranged.

When the referees ask me final questions, I ask them for a couple things I'm planning, whispering and covering my mouth to be certain Assura can't hear or read my lips.

Koviye laughs and claps his hands. "Good luck. She may hate you when you're done."

"She will be too far gone with ecstasy to care," I say, loud enough for her to hear.

Her gaze heats over me with a questioning eyebrow raised. The referees release me to go to her, and the loud chime sounds.

Time to begin.

She stays where she is as I walk to her, and for the first time in hours, I'm allowed to talk to her. My heart is pumping blood so fiercely through my veins, I hear the beats in my ears.

"Are you ready for this?" I ask, my voice hoarse with impatience. The question as much for me as her. I do not think I am ready for this. But I have no willpower to stop myself. Nor can I, with the population of Fellamana watching.

I am on a speeding train and have no idea how to get off. Until I crash.

Her inhales are rapid, and a sleek sheen of perspiration shines over her skin. "It's showtime." She parts the tiny buttons that close the robe between her breasts and her navel.

"We have to fight first," I mutter, almost unthinking, too enamored by watching her fingers to think about any of my plans.

"We will," her voice is low, tuned as though for my

seduction, as if that were necessary. I watch her fingers work, desperate for every inch of skin she exposes. I never knew a belly could be so sexy.

Her movements are so slow, teasing. She's completely aware that every eye is on her, mine as well as thousands of Fellamanas'. She inches the robe off her shoulders.

It is a stunning effect. It silences the crowd, who are quieter than they have been all night.

The gradual revealing of her glorious human skin to all of us is breathtaking. And not just for me. There's an audible gradual gasp from the crowd. Even from afar, the softness, the smoothness of her from head to toe without variation in texture or skin tone, is an anomaly to me and the Fellamana with their varieties of energy colorings.

I wait for us all to soak her in. Then, wanting to see all of her, knowing the crowd will as well, I say, "Turn."

She does, slowly, enjoying the show and our avid attention. She faces me again and does something I do not expect—a backflip, into a handstand.

She makes a circle around me, cartwheeling and tumbling, exhibiting her exquisite strength and flexibility. The crowd, despite their trained manners to remain silent, lets out a gentle clap of appreciation.

She lands in front of me again, out of breath but smiling. "Your turn."

"I have no need to please them." I leave it hanging in the air without saying—*I have only the need to please you.* I cannot bear to say it aloud, but she grasps my meaning.

Her gaze darkens in desire and wanting. "Then what are you waiting for?"

I walk toward her. Her stance is lazy, deceptively so, one hand resting on her cocked hip. A whirring sounds above us, and my first surprise for her comes lowering from the suspension apparatus: a pair of chains, a leather cuff hanging from each.

Her laugh echoes low in her throat. "How the hell are you planning to get me into those?"

"Voluntarily." I step closer. "You will want it."

A growl vibrates from her chest, and fury streams from her eyes. "Never."

It does what I suspected it would. She crouches and launches at me. I'm tackled to the ground. The first step of getting her into those chains.

Chapter Nine

ASSURA

He's a fool. Delusional and pompous.

He lands hard on his back beneath me, so fast the breath is knocked out of him.

"I'd like to see you try," I seethe in his ear, then maneuver him into a headlock.

I don't miss that while I'm on top of him, his cock is steeled in an erection so fierce, it stands forward from his body and gouges into my thigh.

I can't stop myself from rubbing against it, making him moan.

It makes me moan, too, wishing I could ease the ache swelling between my thighs. I'm throbbing. It's unbearable. I want so badly to just fucking fuck him already, godsdamn it. But he had to go and get those handcuffs.

Plus, they want us to demonstrate our fighting foreplay.

Perhaps that's why he did it—the handcuffs—to incite my anger, so we didn't give in to lust too quickly. I won't admit how smart that is. It's too infuriating. It makes me want to bite him, so I do.

I sink my teeth into his ear, and he groans a sound so low, it echoes around me. I'm sure the spectators can hear.

"What's the matter?" I say. "Does your hard-on hurt too much to fight back?" My arm squeezing his throat, holding him to my chest, my breasts lodged against his neck. "You like this pose too much."

His free hand wanders over my hip, his fingers pressing into my thigh. "Not as much as you'll like this one."

He twists my leg, forcing me to let go of him and roll onto my stomach. I have no choice, or he would've dislocated my knee.

"Bastard," I grit. My vulnerable human joints, with no armor, are a serious weakness.

He traps me with his enormous body, straddling my legs and anchoring my wrists. He drags the tip of his cock along the seam of my ass.

I squirm and moan. I can't help it.

His cock is like this aphrodisiac. He does it again, until it almost tickles. It must be torturing him. It makes me arch my pelvis in to him, my body desperately seeking to have him within me.

"You want it," he whispers in my ear. "Admit it. You will do anything to have me inside you again."

I buck beneath him, failing to dislodge him. "Damn you."

"You will even let me put you in those cuffs, if that's what I demand first."

Anger rages in me. I can't let him know how badly he's right. How much my whole body is screaming for him. He hasn't figured out yet that my inner thighs are wet, I'm so ready for him. I've been thinking of nothing but how I want him for the hours we've been watching these cursed Sex Games.

But maybe letting him find out is exactly what I need to do.

I go lax beneath him, soaking in the blissful weight of him over me. It's so easy, I like it so much, I almost fool myself into thinking this is really what I want. "It's true," I whisper.

I chant to myself. *I'm faking it. This isn't how I really feel. It's a ploy.* But it comes too naturally to be false.

He eases his hold on me. "What's true?"

I relax my legs between his, letting them widen, and he lets me, releasing his thighs around my hips. "I'm so wet for you," I plead. "Feel me."

He moves his knees to between mine and glides down between my thighs.

The tip of him hits my opening, dipping into where I'm wettest. The cry of pleasure and longing I let out is not fake.

He swears in a language I don't understand, and his head falls onto my shoulder. "Your cunt is so ready to be fucked." He nudges deeper inside me.

I widen my thighs, slightly, letting him in just an inch.

His hips surge on instinct, his cock butting against me, but my legs aren't open wide enough for him to enter me. A brutal groan sounds from his throat.

I hadn't counted on, or I'd forgotten, how big he is. Just letting him in that small bit has the tip of him butting against my G-spot. It makes me want to come just from him hitting me there.

The pleasure nearly knocks me out, it's so good.

I rock my hips against him, not opening further, just feeling him rub me. The base of his long cock slides between my cheeks and…

Oh…

Something else is nudging the entrance to my ass.

I still. I'd forgotten about that confounded piece of jewelry the Fellamana put around his cock. Those devils. It feels so good, him probing at both my entrances, I almost lose myself.

But not quite. I remember my plan.

His grip on my wrists has loosened enough. Just like I hoped.

"You ready to let me fuck you?" he rumbles, his chest vibrating against my back.

"Not yet." With a surge of strength, I elbow him in the armpit and toss him off me.

I roll away from him and land on my feet. I steady myself in a defensive stance—as best I can when I'm so inflamed; all I really want to do is lie on my back and spread my legs for him.

Nope.

Not yet, anyway. We have to give the crowd the fight demonstration they want.

And I am not letting him put those handcuffs on me, no matter how much I'm dying to be at his mercy. I swore I'd use this time to repay him with pleasure to make up for the pain I've caused another Ssedez.

Soon. I know exactly what the Ssedez needs to feel mindless ecstasy—techniques that on humans would be bitter agony.

He maneuvers into a crouch, and the ferocity in his gaze is unmistakable. So are his fangs, extended brutally past his lower lip.

Gods. I'd get on my knees just to have him bite me. It makes no sense. I don't know why I should want him to bite me, but those fangs drip with something, a venom I bet is an aphrodisiac. I want every pleasure he has to give me.

I shake the thoughts from my head. *Focus!*

He doesn't get up from one knee, his breathing heavy, and his hand sneaks down to squeeze his cock. He winces.

He's in pain. He's so aroused it hurts.

I smirk—he's right where I want him.

He gives a come-at-me gesture. "Give it to me." He can't stand. But he wants me to attack him anyway.

"With pleasure."

I swing a kick at his head, which he blocks, deftly, but he doesn't see my punch to his shoulder until it knocks him on his back.

The surface of the bed is soft. Too forgiving. It's meant for sex, not fighting. I'm unable to pivot fast enough to swing at him again.

I expect him to roll and come up standing, but he lies there, his gold-plated body spread out for me like a meal. Every inch of taut muscle, every hard plane and rigid line is ready and waiting for my taking.

I circle him, stalking him. "Had enough?"

His breath sounds in rapid bursts that aren't fast from physical exertion. It's pure lust. "No," he smiles.

I can't decide if he's lying still because he's too fired with a need for sex to fight back, or if he's playing me. One way to find out.

I lift my foot and prod at his erection with my toes.

He groans in agony and grabs my foot. He swings his leg to knock me off my feet, and I land on my back.

I scuttle to my knees, but he grabs hold of me—one arm binding my arms, the other holding my back against his chest.

I could fight him off. I could twist from his hold, but his hardness against my ass is so fierce, and I need it, crave it. The will to fight drains from my limbs.

"That's it," he breathes and turns his head so mine falls back on his shoulder. It exposes my throat to him. "Is this what you want?" His hot voice drips over my neck.

He scratches his fangs up my throat.

I shudder and arch my neck farther. "Oh gods, please." I want to find out what his bite feels like.

His hand binding my hips releases me, but I have no thought to move. He slips his fingers between my thighs.

I'm aching for it, so the first brush of his fingertip over my clit sends a bolt of excruciating pleasure up my spine. My back bows, and I cry out.

He sucks air through his teeth, and even as he circles my clit and I rotate my hips into his touch, his hand shakes. "Do you surrender?"

I'm tired of fighting. That has to be enough for the crowd.

I just want to give in. To feel what he makes me feel and let him inside me until I'm mindless, flooded with orgasmic euphoria. "Yes."

He takes his hand away, and I whimper from the loss.

But then I hear it, the sound of the chain.

I look to see his hand pull down one of the cuffs hanging from the suspension bar. He lifts my hand and wraps the cuff around my wrist. But he stops. He'll have to release my chest, use both hands to fasten it.

I could fight him off. It would be so easy.

But I don't want to.

"Do it," I whisper, vibrating with anticipation and the explosive need to come, preferably with him buried inside me. I don't want to resist him anymore.

I don't know why, and I'm too out of my mind with lust to care but…I want to be *his*.

He uses both hands to lock the cuff around my one wrist. I lift my other hand, surrendering, letting him bind the other.

The crowd cheers.

Chapter Ten

Gahnin

I stand away from her, and she rests on her knees. Her head is bowed. She stares at the ground, her arms raised overhead, locked to the chains hanging from the suspension rack.

The power in her pose stuns me. I cannot do anything until she lets me. This is not what I expected, but I like it. More than I ever thought I would. I never would've believed something like this, with a human, could be so good.

I stand and face her, watching her.

The crowd is silent, waiting for my next move.

They do not know—it's not *I* who have the next move; it's her.

She inches her head up, until her chin is tilted back, and her gaze drifts hungrily over my cock and rises to my chest. I wait until she meets my eyes.

Air gets trapped in my lungs. Her gaze is the exact look I was hoping for from her, though I hadn't prepared myself for how it would impact me.

Gratitude. Arousal.

She likes it. It turns her on.

"Please," she whispers, so low I almost can't hear her.

"As you command," I murmur with a bow of respect, something I never believed I could feel for her kind. I nod at the referee manning the pulleys on the chains. I wave at him to raise them.

They lift, and Assura stands. She wraps her hands around the chains above the cuffs for handholds.

When her hands are just above her head, but her elbows still bent, I halt the referee. I walk a circle around Assura, trailing fingers lightly up and down her body. Goosebumps sprout on the path of my touch, and she visibly shudders.

I clutch one of her breasts and stop. "Okay?"

She's gasping, her breathing jagged with impatience. "Just—fuck me. Damn you."

I chuckle. Not even with her arms restrained has she relinquished control. She needs something else, then.

I walk over to the props table, and, knowing Assura is watching me, I peruse and make my choice. I hide what I pick up behind my back.

"What is it?" she demands.

I stop in front of her and hold up the black strip of cloth.

"No distractions," I murmur. "I do not want you thinking about the crowd. Only what I make you feel." I wait, giving her the opportunity to refuse.

She sneers, "Bastard," but nods her head just enough to mean "Yes."

I can't help my smile of pride; once again, my guess at what she would like is correct. I take the black strip of cloth I picked up and cover her eyes with it. I tie it in a gentle knot at the back of her head.

I wait for her to get used to the darkness.

She turns her head left and right, searching and failing

to see.

I glide my hands over her sculpted ass, across her hips, and around the front to her ripped abs.

She hums, relishing in the touch of my hands. She leans back against me, arching her breasts, drawing my hands to them. I do as she wants, and she moans with pleasure when I trace her nipples. I circle them, then give them a tight pinch.

She jolts with a sigh.

I do it again, lightly brushing, followed by a tight tug. Then to keep her guessing, I alternate, circling one nipple while pinching the other.

She tightens, her body gathering, her arms straining to hold herself up by her grip on the chains. The sheer strength of her biceps curves into the muscle of her triceps. There is nowhere on her that is not muscled.

When she's gripping so hard that I worry she may come just from my torture of her nipples, I stop and back away.

She groans in frustration.

I make no sound. I want her to wonder where I am, to not be able to guess what I will do next. I walk a slow circle around her.

She turns her head, trying to find me. "Gahnin!"

I hold my breath so she can't hear me. I pause in front of her, far enough she can't feel me, then reach forward and stroke through the curls at the apex of her thighs.

Her knees grow weak, and she's forced to hang on with her hands. She arches her hips in to my touch.

I inhale to ask her to spread her legs, but she does it before I get the words out.

One touch of her soaking wet cunt, and my control shatters. I cannot waste another moment and not taste her. I force my fangs to retract back into my gums and swallow all the venom in my mouth.

I fall to my knees in front of her.

She moans, "Yes," and lifts her leg over my shoulder.

I have barely a moment to take in the sight of her soaked, glistening folds. She's greedy for my cock, for me to make her come. I sink my face between her thighs.

The taste of her, the smell of her, how it makes me want to be inside of her. I need this. I need to eat at her until she screams for me to stop.

I stroke her with my long tongue, feeling into every crevice, tasting every bit of the wetness she has for me. I rub my nose against her hardened clit, and she writhes against my face.

Cries pour from her mouth. "Gahnin! Like that. Yes." They become incomprehensible. The desperate sounds of a woman desperate to climax.

I urge her other leg over my shoulder until she is sitting on me. I hold her to my mouth, digging my fingers into the delectable muscles of her ass cheeks.

I would like to bite those, too.

I snake my tongue as deep inside her as it will go. Her whole body is gathering upward, straining and pulling against her chains. My mouth is in a frenzy, craving the feeling of her cunt spasming in climax.

And then, like I willed it to happen, she does.

She digs her heels into my back and thrusts her hips against my face, and I can't take anymore waiting.

I lower her legs from my shoulders, her thighs still trembling with her climax.

I stand, rewrap her legs around my hips, and bury myself inside her.

She throws her head back and keens a wild noise. Her cunt is still pulsing; it squeezes me, once, twice.

I force myself to thrust through my own orgasm, wanting to make it last. I pour into her in spurts so harsh, she's filled up with me, but there's more.

I cannot stop coming. It's because of the force of the Attachment my body believes it is starting to feel for her. My come overflows onto her thighs, but still I cannot stop thrusting.

She is everything. She is all there is. Her body is my universe. For now.

Eventually, it stops. My hips cease their convulsions. My cock lies still inside her, still hard, but at least the orgasm stopped.

I cling to her. She clings to me. I forget to think there's anything wrong with that. Until she pulls away, I slide out of her, and she rests her feet on the floor.

I'm unstable on my feet and a bit delirious.

She grasps one of my hands over my head, and I do not understand why, until she gets the other one raised as well.

And I look up...

To see my wrists locked in the chains.

Chapter Eleven

ASSURA

The crowd roars.

I have to back away from him, walk it out. My legs are numb, my arms are numb, my body so heated from the roller coaster of orgasms he sent me through, I can barely feel my feet move.

The referees wave to me, assuming that we are finished.

I shake my head and point to Gahnin, where his erection is still protruding from his body. "He's not done, and neither am I." He is far from spent, and I have revenge to enact.

What he did to me—putting me at his mercy like that—and how much I liked it…

Just hanging there, unable to touch him, all I had to do was come. It was the most blissful thing I've ever felt—but still, torture.

It's his turn. I am not a prisoner. I am no one's captive. I am the tormenter. And it's time he knew that. I know things that my past job with the Ten Systems taught me about the

Ssedez body and what it can feel. I know where all the most sensitive places on him are.

But there is one thing first. I don't know what his hard limits are. I have to ask him, "Do you like the chains?"

He snarls at me and refuses to answer.

I point a hard finger at his chest. "Admit you like it, or the referees will take you down."

He inhales a hard breath and grits through his teeth like it's a threat. "I like it."

Triumph, I can't stop from smiling with it. Game on.

I pick up my blindfold that lies on the ground. He tied it so loose that while he was thrusting in me like a man possessed, it fell off.

The haze in his eyes wanes, and he yanks the chains. "How did you get out?" he growls at me, his gaze alight with fury.

I take pleasure in his resistance. "I used to lock people up for a profession. I know how to escape chains."

"What?" He stares at me like he doesn't know who I am. "You'll see."

His arms aren't high enough, since I am slightly shorter than he is. I wave at the referees to raise the chains, and they do. I give him the same courtesy, let his elbows remain slightly bent, so the restraints don't completely lock his joints.

I'm struck motionless staring at his stunning face. I never knew someone's features could be so sharply masculine and yet beautiful at the same time, and not just because of his vividly blue eyes, either. It's something in the sculpting of his cheekbones and the regality of his brow and nose. Those human myths that mistake the Ssedez for immortal deities make perfect sense. And then there's the kissable plushness of his lips...

I will blindfold him, but first, his fangs retracted some time in that last few minutes. I'd like to take advantage of his mouth being free of them. It happens so rarely around me.

I stalk to him, twist a hand in his hair, and yank his mouth to mine.

He smells like me, tastes like me. I like that. This great Ssedez warrior surrendered to me. I am his master now.

His mouth is lush, his lips thick and sucking. He tries to take over the kiss, wrapping his tongue around mine. I like it. I want it. His delectable tongue is starved for more of me. It's all there in his mouth—how if I hadn't restrained him, he'd already be fucking me again.

I pull his head back.

The desire in his blue eyes is molten hot, and the demand in his words is palpable. The way his chest and arms bulge with his hands restrained over his head makes me salivate. I have to make myself wait to feel how hard his muscles are. "Lower the chains. I can't fuck you like this."

"That's because the plan is to fuck *with* you."

He unleashes an animal growl. "Assura. Do it. You want it. Do not make me wait. You do not want to know what will happen if I—"

"Oh yes, I do." I lift the blindfold to his eyes and tie it as tightly around his head as I can. His will not be falling off.

He swears at me in Ssedez. "You will regret this."

I lift my mouth to his ear. "I will enjoy every minute." From the props table, I grab a feather and a knife with a two-inch blade.

Let the torture begin.

The myth about the Ssedez, that they're impervious to everything, is only sort of true. His skin can't be pierced easily, even when his armor isn't out; a Ten Systems blaster laser will glance off his natural armor. No knife, no matter how sharp, will ever draw his blood. But it's like biology forgot something when it reinforced his skin. It's as though by making his skin thicker, it filled it with extra nerve endings, because the Ssedez skin is even more sensitive in some ways than a human's.

I stand behind him and run the feather from the tip of his fingers, down his arm, across his back, then back up the other arm to his fingertips. I do it slowly, and with the moans he makes, you would think I was sucking his cock.

He likes it. I was right.

I kneel in front of him and do the same thing from his toes up his leg. I brush it around his hardness in a light circle, and his knees go partly weak. I trail the feather down his other leg to his toes.

He threatens me. "Now, open your mouth and suck me off."

His cock is at my eye level; it is tempting. I salivate to do exactly as he says, but not on his time.

But I do want to tease him.

"You will like how I taste," he taunts.

I flick my tongue over the tip, then pull back.

His hips buck, and he roars, "Assura! If my hands were free—"

"But they're not, are they?"

He jerks on the chains so hard they rattle. "How the hell did you get out of these things?"

"Not telling."

He wouldn't be able to do it my way, anyway. His wrists are too big to maneuver inside the cuffs like mine could. Plus, I have extra dexterity in my fingers—through practice, of course. I speculate, he likely has no such skill.

I drop the feather and stand in front of him. Close enough that he can feel my breath.

"I know your cunt is aching right now. Let me help." He tilts his head, trying and failing to find a way to see around the blindfold.

I stab his thigh with the knife.

"What the hell?" he shouts, but he doesn't even grimace. The knife can't hurt him, any more than a scratch of the finger on human skin. It won't leave an indentation for more than a second, and the blade can't leave a mark on him.

He lifts a leg and brushes it up my calf.

"Don't touch me," I assert.

It works, though. He puts his foot back on the ground, but now he knows I have a knife.

"What are you planning to do with that?" He's nervous. I wonder if he even knows what kinds of things I can make him feel with a blade.

I set the edge of the knife on his firm, gold pectoral, and he holds his breath.

I put pressure on the blade, and he inhales a ragged breath but remains still, trying not to reveal how it makes him feel. I keep the pressure and drag the blade across his chest. It leaves no visible mark on his skin.

His jaw falls open, and he makes a guttural sound in the back of his throat. It's hard to know if it's a sound of pain or pleasure, so I stop. I lift the blade from his chest.

His breath gasping, "Again," he whispers with a note of shock in his tone.

I smile. He didn't know. I'm making him feel new things, that he likes.

I set the blade to a different spot on his pec and draw it across again. I increase the pressure as I go. His sounds escalate to moans, and I don't stop.

I'm elated, and for the first time in a long time, I feel a lightness in my chest. A softening of the burden of guilt I've carried. Surely, making him feel pleasure like this can erase some of my crimes.

I keep going. I make stripes with the blade across him, moving downward, though it leaves no mark. It's like scratching across leather. I skip his nipples and move to his abs. I increase the pressure with every swipe.

His skin shows no indentation, no change in coloring from where I've touched him. My pressure gets harsh enough that, on a human, it would scrape their skin off.

But by the time I reach his navel, his body is wracking so hard with ecstasy that he starts to orgasm. He spurts onto me as I stand in front of him.

I look down, and I'm stunned. By two things.

His come is silver. It glistens on my pale skin like he's coated me in molten metal.

But even more surprising is what's happened to the tip of his cock. The gold armor of his skin has peeled back. Just an inch; it's not much, but what it exposed beneath looks more tender than human skin.

"Don't…let them…see," he whispers, amid his climax, and there's a note of panic in his voice.

If I stabbed him with the knife there, I would without a doubt pierce him. I've found the one and only true point of weakness where the Ssedez natural armor is vulnerable to a blade.

I never discovered this in my torture. I never made a Ssedez orgasm from my knife skills. Though I never set out to make it feel good, either. It makes a difference. The things I did were the minimum of what I was ordered to do.

My heart accelerates over what Gahnin's secret means. The Ten Systems military doesn't know about the Ssedez's vulnerability in the state of arousal. No one does.

I hide the tip of his cock with my hand.

"Thank you," he gasps and keeps coming against my hand.

I'm dying to taste him, so I drop to my knees and take him into my mouth.

The sensation of him in my mouth is exquisite. He's spilling onto my tongue, a flavor so rich, I suck on him, trying to draw out more.

"Yeah, like that," he groans and thrusts into my mouth, the chains jangling above his head.

I swallow and keep swallowing, until he's flooded my mouth, and his silver come is dripping onto my chin. But I want more. It has an addictive quality. The more I get, the more I crave.

It makes me feel how empty I am to my core. I'm aching between my legs, dying to be fucked there, the way he is doing my mouth.

But I can't stop, either. I can't bring myself to take my mouth away. Luckily, he makes the decision for me.

Somehow, he managed to get out of the cuffs. It seems I'm not the only one good with locks.

He grabs my shoulders and tosses me onto my back.

I bounce on the soft surface and land with my legs spread wide. I reach for him. "Gahnin!"

He wrenches off his blindfold, then he is over me and gorging himself inside me with ceaseless abandon.

I don't know how much longer he will last. I hope he never stops.

But more, I hope he never finds out how I knew the way to make him feel all those things I did.

Chapter Twelve

GAHNIN

I wake the next morning in a strange bed without her.

My body is confused. I reach for her, already hard, straining for her again. Expecting her to be there, like last night, hungry and dying to be fucked, the way I like to give it to her.

I am a Ssedez obsessed. I do not know what is happening to my body.

It was absurd and ridiculous how many times we orgasmed on that stage.

In the end, the referees had to tell us to stop. We were declared the prestigious winners by a record-breaking margin, and Koviye informed us we achieved our goal of winning the Fellamana's respect. The sheer number of times we orgasmed alone was enough to put us above the competition, to say nothing of the spectacle we put on.

It was like a contest between her and I, neither wanting to give in and show satisfaction to the other.

What I suspected is true. With her body at full strength, she can take as much as I can give. I want her again so badly, it hurts.

But she's not here.

I flop onto my back, cover my eyes, and swear.

These godsdamn Fellamana and their games. I did not get her out of my system. The *desidre* feels no less. It hurts more than ever. And this forsaken Attachment leaching through my veins... My fangs are throbbing so much; my head is pounding. Everything is worse. So much worse, I wish I could go back in time and let Pvotton take my place in the cell with her.

A tone so low that it resonates through the walls fills the room. It takes me a minute to realize—it's me. I am growling like a crazed beast. The strength of my visceral reaction forces me to admit Pvotton taking my place was never an option.

Damn, what she did to me...

How did she know a knife would make me feel like that? I did not know a blade across my skin would feel so good, or that it could make me come.

I wonder if this is something many Ssedez do, and I have just missed it because I have only ever had one lover, my mate.

Tiortan. A well of emotion floods my chest, and I cover my face with my hands. I do not know what to do with myself, with all the certainties of my past that are being erased by the present, with what I am feeling for this human that is a tragedy of catastrophic proportions.

There has to be a way to stop this. The Attachment is spreading in me. My body has already fallen. My heart is on its way. My soul will be next, if I can't stop it. All it takes after that is a willingness to sacrifice my life for hers—and the Attachment will be complete on my side.

I will never bite her, and so my venom will never cause her to grow fangs and return my bite, as Nemona did for Oten.

Therefore, no threat of her ever forming the Attachment for me exists, but the respect I began to feel for her last night has not diminished. It has grown.

I...can't believe it... I actually...like her.

She was impressive last night. Her tricks with the knife were too good to be guesses. Doing that to a human would skin them alive. It was like she knew how it would affect me. Like she'd done it before.

I bolt up in bed.

She's been with a Ssedez before.

My fangs are dripping with venom, and a possessive need to do violence storms through my body. Whoever the Ssedez was, I will kill them.

Oh gods.

I shake myself. What the hell is wrong with me?

But I cannot stop seeing it. If she has been with another Ssedez, I need to know who. I have not left her since she entered this town, so it did not happen here. It must have been while she was with the Ten Systems. Though I do not know how, since the humans have believed we were extinct for the past hundred years.

I have to find out.

I launch from bed, naked, and find my leather pants and boots. I dress, grateful I never again have to see that strap contraption the Fellamana put me in.

I look around and see for the first time I'm in a room with opaque walls.

The Fellamana actually gave me some privacy for the night. Or maybe they wanted to block my view of Assura, so that I would not try to fuck her again in my sex-crazed state.

I'm determined to find her now.

I throw the door open and storm into the hall. "Where is she?" I bellow.

My warriors, all nine of them, are outside my door. They

are a lineup of gold muscle, strapped with weapons and ready for duty. They stare at me like they have never seen me before.

I freeze in horror, cover my mouth, and turn my back. It is bad enough I had my fangs out last night for them to see during the competition. For me to have them out now is akin to an adolescent lacking control over his hormones.

I grit my teeth, think of innocuous non-sensual things, like weapons and knives...

Not knives.

Trees and flowers and plants and gradually, my fangs withdraw into my gums. I force myself to take a calming breath and turn back around to my warriors.

They all politely stare at the ceiling or the floor, pretending they did not notice my obscene faux pas of having my fangs out in public.

"Commander." Pvotton steps forward and speaks in Ssedez as though nothing out of the ordinary has happened. "We're ready to travel to the *Origin* crash site." Hearing my own language snaps my attention back to reality better than anything.

I glance out a window at the end of the hall and see the sun high in the sky. "How long have you been out here?"

"Hours," Anewtan says down the lineup. Her voice is dry with frustration. Grunts of agreement from the others echo her.

If I could feel embarrassment, I would. Shirking duty because I'm recovering from having sex with a human for hours in front of everyone—that's...shaming. That they all believed me in mourning before they saw it is worse.

I clear my throat and stand taller. I have the urge to explain my behavior, to apologize for my appalling lateness. But I cannot think of what to say. I cannot say aloud that even though I am supposed to still be in mourning for another century and humans killed my mate, I am forming the Attachment for one. They already see it. My fangs would not be out if it were not true. It's shameful. They have every right to judge me for my lack of respect for Tiortan.

They don't show it on their faces and hide their outrage well. Saying nothing will be better than admitting how out of control of myself I am.

Yet the burning shame I feel standing in front of them is overwhelmed by the burning need to get back to Assura. I shove both feelings away, as my duty requires, and give my warriors the stare of authority they're used to from me.

They watch my transformation and respond, straightening themselves, and there's an almost audible sigh of relief among them. Too many days of leisure have weighed on all of us. We are more comfortable with discipline. That is our way of life.

Two days would have been enough. Four is too long. They are anxious for duty. That's why they are here.

I need the same. My fixation on Assura stops, now.

"Pvotton, find Koviye," I order.

"Yes, sir." He stiffens to attention in gratitude and goes down the hall.

"The rest of you, wait outside. Take your leave of any Fellamana you see and express your gratitude for their hospitality." I glance down the long end of the hallway. "I will find the human."

"Sir," Anewtan steps forward again. "I would do that for you." There's force in her words and nods from the others.

They do not trust me alone with Assura. I do not trust myself, either. But I cannot let go of the fervent need to speak with her. I have to know who is the other Ssedez she knows intimately. "I will do it."

A few of them give me skeptical looks, but I order, "We leave in half an hour." They turn and go in the opposite direction from me.

I search through the rooms and find them empty. I open

a door to a stairwell and hear voices. One of them is Assura's.

I launch up the steps, three at a time, exit through a door, and come to a halt.

She's talking to a Fellamana female and wearing one of those clinging white suits. Her weapons belt she arrived with is strapped around her hips.

Her gaze begins with annoyance at the interruption but quickly morphs to something else once she sees me. Her eyes wander down my chest, and she shifts on her feet. I know that posture. It's the same one she had while waiting for me on the stage last night.

My erection is trapped by my leather, and I cannot forget the question I need to ask her. In private.

"We have to talk." I suspect she will protest.

Her breathing visibly accelerates, her breasts rising and falling. Her nipples are hardened beneath her suit. "Fine."

She turns and walks down the hall.

I follow her, until we are out of sight of the Fellamana woman. The hall is empty, and I have no patience for getting inside a room.

I grasp her shoulder and steer Assura toward a wall.

She tries to ask, "What are you—"

But I trap her against the wall. My chest molded to her back, her body pressed to mine, I'm helpless not to run my hands down her hips and thighs.

She could fight me off, kick me, head-butt me, but she doesn't. She groans and softens, her body accepting my weight. She rubs her ass against me, feeling how hard I am for her.

"Still haven't had enough?" I breathe in her ear.

"Fuck you," she bites in a whisper but sighs as I start to rub back against her, easing and stoking the physical ache and the clawing need to be inside her again.

"How did you know about the knife?" I grit between my

teeth, though I am unable to stop moving against her.

"What are you talking about?" But she stiffens.

I grasp her hands. "Tell me. How did you know a knife would make me come like that? How did you know a Ssedez would do that?"

"I didn't," she protests, but it's a moan. She releases her arms to me, and I anchor her hands to the wall beside her head.

"You have been with a Ssedez before. Who?"

"None of your business."

"You admit it!" I snap, but I am so hard, my cock pulsates against her ass. I have to be inside her.

"I admit nothing."

"Who was it?" I hiss in her ear.

"I'm not telling you."

Anger bursts in my chest. My fangs are out, demanding to claim her vein, to make her feel so much pleasure, she never has eyes for another but me again. I drag the sharp points along her jaw. "Did you fuck him?"

"No," she moans, breathless.

"You just made him come." Which is worse, I do not know. My brain is too fogged with the one-track thought that, *She is mine. Must be inside her so she knows it.*

"No."

I growl an animal sound of approval. I believe her. Though why I have learned to trust the word of a human, I do not understand. "What *were* you doing?"

She ignores me and taunts, "What would you do if I said I had sex with him?"

I press her harder against the wall with the full force of my weight. "I'd make you come so hard, you'd forget him."

Her breath shudders. "Then, I fucked him." She has no idea what her saying those words does to me, even though I know she's lying.

It provokes the possessive beast in me so fiercely, I start to shake. "You want me inside you so badly, you would lie?"

"How do you know I wasn't lying the first time, that it isn't true?"

I snarl in her ear. "Sneaky bitch."

"The sneaky bitch you want so bad, you've forgotten she's your worst enemy."

I have enough rationality left to think I should deny her. If she wants me badly enough to provoke me like this, the best torture would be to leave her unsatisfied. But it would be torture for me, too.

"Are you scared?" she mocks.

"I'm scared of nothing."

"Then shut up and fuck me." She arches against me, like a cat in heat.

I grit my teeth and fail to remember that her being my worst enemy isn't even more of a reason to bang her senseless.

Her voice comes out keening and desperate. "Do I have to beg?"

"Yes." I want her to.

"Please, Gahnin," she whispers desperately. The need in her voice cuts through my resistance. I'm incapable of leaving her wanting like this.

I pull at the back panel of her suit. My fingers shake, unable to find a zipper somewhere, anywhere. I'm an instant away from ripping the fabric. Panting, she unbuckles her weapons belt, drops it on the floor with a clang, and reaches for buttons.

She wrenches it open, and her sumptuous ass is exposed.

I swear, staring and yanking at my fly. It's like her suit was made to give me access to her. Knowing the Fellamana, it probably was.

She spreads her legs, props her bottom in the air, presenting herself to me. "Hurry." She bounces, making the firm muscles jiggle.

I groan, pull out my cock. And thrust inside her.

We both cry out. I grip her hips, digging myself as deep in her as I can go. She's so wet, it's like all the come I filled her with last night is still inside her. Probably is.

She rocks her hips, greedy for me to move. I do. I drive into her so hard, my skin slaps against hers. I do it again and spread her cheeks so I watch my cock sink inside her.

It exposes her other opening, and wanting to torture her more, I press my thumb to it.

"Yes," she moans low in her throat, and I press harder.

She's so wanton for everything I give her, I want her to beg for it more.

I drive into her, fast, her body shaking with the force of my lust. Her hands press against the wall to keep her upright.

She keens in her throat. But her cunt—her insatiable, velvet, soaked cunt—does not spasm around me. All the other times she has started to orgasm by now.

Because I'm not pressing the spot in her front she loves so much. But I want to punish her for lying to me. For thinking she could manipulate me.

For succeeding.

I lean forward and growl in her ear, "Touch yourself." Her eyes fall closed, and she drags her palm down the wall.

I resume my thrusting, intending to make it as hard for her as I can, wanting her to work for it. But her hand disappears between her legs, and I see her arm moving, performing the circles I know she needs.

She tightens around me, her ass arching into me.

I have a thought that I want this to last. That I will not get to do this again. Once we leave here, we will go back to our duty, and I will not touch her anymore.

But it's as though the thought makes me more desperate for her, makes me more aware of her, makes it feel better, sharper, clearer.

I orgasm, pleasure shooting through my nerves like sparks, short-circuiting my brain, as though I will never think again.

She climaxes around me, the force of my thrusts aiding her. I pump into her in aftershock spasms. My reflex inserting every drop of come I have into her. Then we're still, the only sound our breathing…

…and other people talking around the corner of the hall. One of them with a Ssedez accent.

Damn it.

They had to have heard us. Or even seen us. I jerk away from her, backing up until I hit the opposite wall. This is insanity. After how many times last night and the night before, I'm so mindless for her, I do her in a hallway without any thought of onlookers.

She does not look at me. She keeps facing the wall and bends down to pick up her weapons.

That she dropped them like that…no warrior treats their weapons so carelessly. She searches them, inspecting them, obviously shocked she tossed them.

Her voice chimes low and guttural, harsh with warning. "We're not doing this again."

It feels like I'm gouging out my chest to say it, but that is all the more reason why I should. "No, we are not."

Chapter Thirteen

Assura

I'm still breathing hard, still unable to put my legs together, I'm so tender. But I can't look at him.

I examine my blasters, check my explosives and my knives, exasperated. So careless. My weapons are my life, my first line of defense when under attack. I treat them with respect.

Not like a pair of socks!

At least the voices in the hall have stopped, and we're alone now. We must have been loud enough to scare them away.

His tone is subdued. "We leave for the *Origin* crash site in ten minutes."

"Okay." His come is seeping down my thighs, so I can't close up the "fuck panel" in my suit. That's my new name for it. Because that's obviously what it's for.

I thought it was just for taking a piss.

Apparently not.

"I have to clean up, then I'll be down." I'm not traipsing through the jungle today with a soggy suit reminding me with every step how I begged him this morning.

Damn it.

I am a soldier. Not a fuck buddy for a Ssedez. I don't care if I'm supposed to be making things right with his species after the crimes I've committed. It does not shirk me of my duty. We're getting back to the *Origin* today.

"Why do you need to clean..." he whispers, then obviously sees his copious amounts of silver come glistening on my thighs. "Oh. Right."

Sick of him staring at my ass, I turn around. "From here on out, I am a soldier to you and no more. Got it? I am not even female. If I catch you staring at me, talking to me, or treating me like we've had sex before, I will..."

I'll... What? Stab him with a knife? I can't. His skin won't allow it.

Kill him? As if I'd light him on fire.

But there has to be something I can threaten him with. "I'll..." Then I remember his secret I learned last night. How he asked me to hide the vulnerable tip of his cock when he ejaculated on me. It's cruel, but the potential he has to harass me for what has happened between us, combined with how little I trust him, rationalizes it.

"I'll tell Jenie and every surviving member of the *Origin's* crew about the Ssedez's weakness in their armor."

His nostrils flare, and he glares fire at me. "You would not. You have more honor than that."

"I do. But I have less trust for you. You treat me with the respect I deserve, and you won't have a problem. Otherwise..." I leave the threat hanging in the air.

"You think so little of me?" He steps closer. "You think I'm so without integrity that I would treat a female warrior as lesser?"

"I don't know you. I have no idea what you're like with females except when you're fucking them." Every Ten Systems military male I know, if they'd found out I was female, likely would've tried. Their jokes and dialogue betrayed it. That's why we wore armor and helms at all times to hide our gender, along with voice scramblers.

He straightens. "Your Ten Systems army was cruel."

"Duh. We had no choice. Once the Ten Systems deemed me soldier material, forcing me to take tests I didn't want to, I became their slave. Rebellion was the only way out. That's why our group risked our lives to escape." He doesn't need to know that it was pretty much due to my plan and action that we escaped. That I succeeded only so far as to get us away, and not to free General Dargule's prisoners, including one Ssedez who, after over a hundred years of captivity, is still chained to a wall aboard the military starship, the *Hades.*

He gives a heavy sigh and glances at the floor. "There are female warriors among my Ssedez. If you require reassurance, they would gladly answer your concerns." He lifts his eyes to me. "But I swear to you, I will not treat you ill for what has happened between us. And if I do, I would expect no less than for you to reveal the Ssedez secret."

Hearing him say it relieves a tension binding my chest. I take a deep breath. I want to believe him but don't know if I should.

His face softens, and he grasps my shoulders. "Assura, you have my respect as a warrior."

"What about as a human?"

He jerks back from me like I've poisoned him. "Humans killed my mate. I will never have respect for your species."

I don't know what slogs me harder in the chest: the fact that he had a mate, the fact that she's dead, the fact that humans killed her. "I'm sorry."

He stiffens, his whole body hardening in a way I've not

seen. A coldness enters his eyes, but he doesn't respond.

He walks away, saying over his shoulder, "You have five minutes."

The trek through the jungle has me on edge. I'm plagued by memories of when I was struggling, wounded and alone, burning with the fever of the *desidre*. I was also injured with a stab wound that would've been fatal if I hadn't had the escape pod's emergency supplies. Those didn't save me from infection, but they stopped the bleeding so I didn't die.

Enormous trees like something out of Earth's Jurassic period span as far as the eye can see. A quarter mile into the jungle, and all signs of the Fellamana town disappear.

A group of seventeen, we trek up a road, then cut onto a single-track dirt trail. The vigorous undergrowth blanketing the ground in plants with blue, purple, and green leaves brush our legs as we walk.

The suit the Fellamana gave me keeps the plants from cutting into my skin. Unlike the suit I arrived with, which was in tatters by the time I found my way out of the jungle.

Animals chirp and buzz in the trees overhead, but all of them are hiding in the foliage.

The group of Ssedez warriors chat alongside the Fellamana. The Fellamana each wear enormous packs on their backs that I assume contain supplies for my friends. Many of the Ssedez seem to have learned far more of the Fellamana language than I've managed to, but I console myself that they had time to do so while I was unconscious in the hospital.

Gahnin speaks quietly in the lead with his second in command, Pvotton.

I chat with Anewtan, one of the female Ssedez warriors,

taking Gahnin up on his suggestion to ask about how their culture treats female warriors.

"We are of much value," she says. Her attire is no different from the Ssedez males, except for a leather bra she wears, which seems to function for support and no more. Her skin is as glittering gold in the sunlight as her male counterparts'. "There are many leadership skills and tactics that a Ssedez female may possess in greater strength than a male."

I'm grateful to talk to another female for the first time in over a week. I'm eager to see Jenie and anyone else who has survived. There are many names I'd mourn if I learn they are gone. "How come so many of the Ssedez know the human language?"

"We spend our entire military training studying everything we know about the Ten Systems, including your language."

"I'm grateful you're helping us," I say, still surprised they seem to have buried their hatred of our species so easily.

"Our commander tells us we made a mistake in attacking your rebellion. He is mated to your General Nemona now." She steps over a large tree, and I follow.

"They're mated, like forever?" I can't really fathom that. Committing a lifetime to someone, I don't know what that looks like. Spending an eternity with Gahnin...

My breath stops, and I have to let the thought go to start breathing again.

"Yes, forever," Anewtan confirms. "He bit her, and she turned Ssedez."

"What?" I stop walking. "She turned into a Ssedez? Just from him biting her?"

Anewtan pauses and looks back at me. "I believe he bit her many times, but yes, our venom seems to have that effect on humans. She is now gold of skin with a dexterous Ssedez tongue and has lovely fangs of her own."

Nemona is now not only mated to a Ssedez, but she *is* one. I start walking again and run my tongue over my teeth just thinking what that would be like.

"I believe it was an accident," she says. "It is not normal for a Ssedez to bite a non-Ssedez."

A wild ecstatic thought occurs to me. "Did Nemona also get your natural armor?"

"I believe so."

To be invincible like that, to never be harmed by a blaster or a blade again… I'm now even sorrier Gahnin refused to bite me. I suppose that was why—he didn't want to make one of his enemies invincible.

Anewtan says quietly, so no one around us can hear, "You know what it means that Gahnin's fangs come out when he's near you, right?"

"He's turned on by me." I surmised that on my own. I don't know why she thinks that's not obvious. She doesn't respond. "Gahnin said his mate died. How long ago was that?"

"Tiortan died in the final year of the war with the Ten Systems. She was aboard a civilian cruiser that the Ten Systems destroyed."

"Oh." That explains a lot of Gahnin's anger toward me. I pause to do that math. "But that was over a hundred years ago." More than a human lifetime.

"The Ssedez live near a thousand years. For him to only mourn Tiortan for such a short time is…well…" Her voice gets tight. "On our home world, it would be very shocking, but this planet, Fyrian, is making us all do strange things we would not normally do."

I frown at the back of her head. Her implication that Gahnin had sex with me only because of the *desidre* is… sort of true, I guess. But it wrenches my heart to hear it that way. He could've chosen anyone; he could've found someone else to help me feed my *desidre*, but he didn't. He chose to do it himself, so Anewtan can make excuses for him all she likes. He's attracted to me, despite me being human, despite humans killing his mate.

Whoa, it suddenly really hits me what that means. He must be attracted to me like...a lot. As if I didn't know that really. I'm still achingly, erotically sore; that's how well I know it.

Koviye comes to walk beside me, his expression and voice grave, full of a seriousness I've never seen from him. "Did Gahnin tell you?"

"He's not speaking to me." Which, now I know about his mate's death at the hands of humans, I wonder he'll ever speak to me again. My lungs spasm on my breath, and I have to cough it out. I don't want that. I don't want this to be over between us.

But am I really expecting us to have contact without wanting to have sex? No.

We have a mission. A ship to repair, a crew to recover, and...who knows what host of other problems wait for us there. Those are priority.

I almost expect Koviye to make a remark about my sexual relationship with Gahnin, but he surprises me.

He almost ignores my mention of Gahnin. "You should know, the Fellamana scanners tracked an unidentified ship orbiting our planet."

A chill runs over my skin. "What do you mean 'unidentified'? As in you don't recognize it, or as in there are no markings?"

"As in there are no markings. It's flying under stealth. The only reason we even know it's there is because our satellite is transmitting an image."

My heartbeat accelerates, and I have to remind myself to breathe. No reason to overreact yet. I school my voice to remain calm. "Can I see the image?"

He pulls a vid from a pocket in his uniform that he donned in place of a robe, which now I think about it, resembles the Ten Systems uniform with its gray panels and black piping. "Here."

On the screen is a live image from space. The Fellamana planet, red as fire due to the *desidre* toxin in the atmosphere, is a curve on the edge of the screen, but in the center is a starship. A warship. An ebony, glistening, unmarked, Ten Systems ship. That I recognize like it's my own.

"Dargule," I whisper, and my heart flies in my chest. I have to stop walking and center myself.

"Assura, what's wrong?" Koviye asks.

I start to see spots, and I have to close my eyes and count my breaths and talk myself out of my panic. Dargule is not actually here yet. He's still in space. He may never come down and enter the atmosphere.

Koviye calls out to the others, and everyone is bustling around me.

"Assura, what is it?" Gahnin's heavy voice sounds in front of me, and I absurdly, maddeningly, take comfort in him being there.

I reach my hand out. I don't even have to open my eyes to know it's shaking.

Gahnin takes my hand and whispers, "You recognize the ship?"

"The *Hades*." I open my eyes and meet his. "I used to live on it."

We race up the trail as fast as our feet will move. It gets steeper.

I juggle Koviye's radio in my hand, trying every signal, calling, "Jenie, come in. Jenie, can you hear me?" at every station. Koviye communicates with the Fellamana in town on his commlink, telling them to hunker down and prepare for a possible attack.

I'm consumed with guilt. The Fellamana are an isolated, peace-loving species, and we have brought the Ten Systems on them. There's no doubt Dargule found some way to track the *Origin*. Some way that I didn't think of.

And we're all going to pay for it, with our lives.

I give up on the radio. Jenie must have no signal systems set up. They have no reason to. We're alone in our rebellion. We have no one to communicate with.

"I'm sorry," I say to Koviye between panting breaths, my feet padding as fast as they'll go on the trail.

"Don't be," he says, and I swear there's a smile in his voice. "We've been preparing for this day for a long time."

I don't have the heart to tell him his people don't stand a chance against the *Hades* if Dargule decides to destroy them.

"Just because we don't fight," Koviye says, "doesn't mean we don't know how to defend ourselves from the Ten Systems. We may be isolated, but we're not stupid."

Not wanting to crush his hopes, I don't respond. There is no scenario in my imagination where the peace-loving, no-tolerance-for-violence Fellamana survive an attack from the *Hades*.

In front of me, Gahnin passes me a look over his shoulder. He's thinking what I'm thinking: we're all screwed.

We're racing to get to Jenie and the surviving crew, to warn them. They have no satellite imagery to tell them the *Hades* is orbiting around us right now. Though how the warning will help them, I don't know. If Dargule decides to enter the atmosphere, to attack us from the air, we have no capability to fight the *Hades*'s weapons system.

The *Origin* had the defenses to fight back, but she's in pieces. Pieces big enough for the *Hades* to view from space. They're likely just circling until they find the crash site. Then they'll destroy what's left of us.

"How far away are your Ssedez ships?" I ask Gahnin, out of breath. I don't want to bring his people into this, either, but I have to ask.

"Too far." His voice is subdued. He knows this is bad. Very bad.

Koviye says behind me, "You must relax and believe me. The Fellamana have our ways. We will protect you all. You will be safe." His voice seems unlabored by the run.

"What are you planning?" I ask.

"You will see."

Not wanting to argue, I roll my eyes and move on. Let him cling to his delusions if it gives him hope. It's not my job to crush his naïve optimism.

We reach the outskirts of the *Origin* crew's temporary camp, and the others wait on the edge of the jungle, where the guards to the camp can't see them.

Since I'm the only one they know, it's best I go forward alone.

Koviye marches up beside me. "I'll come with you."

"I don't think that's wise." I don't pause in my run, though. Time is too urgent for me to slow and argue with him.

"Jenie knows me. We've been introduced."

If the situation weren't so dire, I'd probably laugh. "Good luck to you. I hope you don't get shot with a laser."

"I'm with you. They won't shoot me."

"The only person here who will recognize me without my armor and credentials is Jenie." Gods, now I think about it, I hope *I* can get past the guards.

We reach a break in the trees and come to a village of temporary metal structures. I'm glad to see it. They obviously salvaged a lot from the *Origin's* wreckage. They should have stockpiled weapons as well.

Not that they'd help against the *Hades,* but if Dargule

actually lands his ship and tries to wage battle with us in person, we'd be able to fight back. Though in any case, I doubt it will last long. There's no reason why he shouldn't just blast this whole place from his ship, killing us all.

Well, there's one reason—me.

He'd want to see the fear on my face as he captures me. He's *that* sort of evil. And if he did, if he landed the *Hades*, I could sneak aboard. Because there are other people on board that ship. People who need my help. The people who I'd promised I'd save and then never did.

This could be my chance to free them from the cages in the bowels of Dargule's ship. My excitement makes my feet go faster.

The first guard I see is female. She's dressed in a Ten Systems informal uniform, the gray with black piping on the sides. It's all we had to wear after launching our rebellion. We'd had no time or resources to make new uniforms, so we ripped the Ten Systems logo patches off our existing ones.

She brightens on seeing me. "Hey, did you just come in off an escape pod?" She puts up a hand to halt my steps.

I stop. "I need to find Jenie. Do you know where she is?"

"Who are you?" She glances curiously at Koviye on my other side.

I almost don't want to tell her who I am. She'll know me by reputation. Every person in the thousand-member crew knows my name. "Assur." I say my gender-neutral name she knows, that the Ten Systems assigned me, and then follow up with my fifteen-digit ID number, known only to crew. "It's actually Assura."

She quickly checks my ID on a nearby computer, and then her expression changes to one of pure joy, and though I don't recognize her, she shrieks with excitement. "You're alive!"

I bypass her jubilation. "There's an emergency. Please take me to Jenie."

"Right." She asks no more questions and runs ahead, leading the way.

We pass lots of crew who wave hello. I recognize none of their faces since I'm used to seeing them only obscured behind helms and armor, which I'm happy to see no one is wearing anymore. I'm overjoyed to discover as we move past them that such a large number of our rebel crew are women, though there are some men in the group.

I don't know why I never figured it out before. I guess we were all pretending so hard to protect ourselves, we even fooled one another.

The guard leads me into a three-sided shelter and stops with a salute. "General Jenie, Assura is here."

"What?!" I hear a cry in surprise and recognize Jenie's voice.

A thrill goes down my spine, and I step around to see Jenie's beautiful, radiant face. I can't help it; I start to cry.

"Jenie," I choke.

She walks toward me, and tears cloud her eyes, too. "Assura, my love."

She embraces me, and it's the homecoming I've needed since crash-landing on this planet. Of all the times in the jungle I thought I would die and never see her again, here she is. Her arms are warm and her comfort welcoming. I can't not give her a kiss.

She rests her forehead against mine and whispers, "You came back."

"I promised you before, I'm impossible to kill."

She laughs and hugs me again. It's what I told her before I went alone to plant the bomb in the Ten Systems space station that created our diversion to escape.

I haven't admitted to her that I stole one of Dargule's prized experimental weapons in my failed attempt to free the prisoners.

She stiffens in my arms. "Koviye?"

I pull back. "You know him?"

She's staring at the Fellamana over my shoulder with a note of astonishment. The joy that had transformed her face on seeing me fades, and in its place forms a bright red blush so hot, her cheeks look like someone took pink paint to them. "What are you doing here?"

Koviye gives her his worst, or I guess best, flirtatious smile and a slight bow. "It is a pleasure to see you again, General Jenie."

She straightens her shoulders, obviously not certain what to say, and her jaw grinds. Which for Jenie is strange. She's not socially awkward; she's articulate and self-assured and...

She's totally attracted to him.

I can't help a soft chuckle. I don't know what happened between them before, but I can't blame her, really. His joviality would do her good.

As much as I enjoyed sharing a bed with her on occasion, I've never felt possessive of her, always wanting her to find pleasure with whomever she chooses. I miss the easygoing-ness of this relationship.

This thing with Gahnin and all the possessive, fierce, consuming lust is something completely new and overwhelming and...

Never happening again.

I have to stop myself from smacking the side of my head to get the thoughts to end.

Koviye puts a hand over his heart, or where a human heart would be, and says sincerely, "I hate to interrupt this beautiful reunion, but there is a source of impending death over our heads."

Jenie squints at him. "What are you talking about?"

I touch her arm, drawing her attention to me. "They found us."

Chapter Fourteen

GAHNIN

It takes too long for Assura to come back. Pvotton talks nonstop caution in my ear, telling me to wait and not be rash and go after her.

He's giving me concerned looks, too. All the Ssedez are.

I'm pacing and acting like a male who's entered the second stage of the Attachment—where I would be no longer just physically Attached to her, but emotionally as well. As though my emotions for her are inhibiting my reason.

I cannot see past my obsession of getting to her. It's no longer about sex and just my physical need to mate with her. It's turned deeper. Like I am invested in her. Like her well-being matters to me.

I feel like my insides have been ripped open. Feeling this…this…whatever it is for her is tearing holes in the very fabric of me. It should not be possible. And yet, it is happening. I can no longer deny it. I am forming the Attachment for her.

I do not know how to stop it—if it can be stopped. I have

to somehow. I owe another century of mourning to Tiortan's memory. I cannot think of Attaching to anyone until then, least of all a human.

The terror on Assura's face when she saw the image of the *Hades* wrenched something open in me. I cannot abandon her. I would rather die. Which is...shocking. And has me pulling on my hair so hard, I am in danger of ripping it from my skull.

Anewtan pulls me aside, grabbing my arm. "You haven't bitten her yet, right?"

"No, of course not," I snap.

She nods emphatically. "Have you tried to save her life?"

"What?" I don't understand her question.

"Have you irrationally tried to save Assura's life, endangering yours in the process?"

"No," I growl. "She takes care of herself."

She slaps my back so hard, I give a grunt. "Good. As long as you don't do those things and you don't turn her Ssedez like Oten did to Nemona, no matter how rampant your feeling for her, the Attachment will not complete itself. You are still in control of what happens."

She's right. No matter how far gone my body and emotions are, as long as I never bite her or try to sacrifice my life for hers, I'm safe. For the Ssedez female to Attach, it is even easier. She need not willingly sacrifice herself for her male, merely bite him and give her heart, soul, and body to him—though that is hardly a simple thing.

I remember doing it for Tiortan. The Ssedez have made the last part of the Attachment a ritual, which couples formally agree to once they freely choose to finalize the biological mating. They arrange for a scenario, a surprise fake scenario, where the couple who has begun to form the Attachment must "risk their life" to save the other.

Many get very creative. There's always a safety net, of

course. No one would actually die, but when you're in the throes of the initial stages of the Attachment, you're not thinking rationally enough to know that. The ritual forces us to admit just how important the other is to us. And that admission cements the Attachment into a lifelong bond.

No one's going to do a Ssedez ritual for me Attaching to a human. I would have to complete the Attachment on my own. I won't. "I can still control myself."

Anewtan hardens her tone. "You're still in mourning, Gahnin. The fact that you have let your feelings go so far for this human is shameful to Tiortan."

It is like she reached into my chest and pulled my heart out. I have to close my eyes to cope with the pain. I am glad she said it. She's right. Were I home among our people, having sex with someone else after only one century of mourning would be taboo, and others would think much less of me. It is so rare among the Ssedez.

The shame clears my thoughts, refreshes my mind so I'm able to think clearly for the first time since I felt the *desidre*. "It is true." I am Ssedez, and that comes before any irrational feelings caused by an alien world. I cannot abandon our sacred traditions. I cannot love a human, a race that robbed Tiortan and countless other Ssedez of their lives.

Anewtan grasps my arm. "Do not lose hope. I know you have been alone for nigh a century, but someday, when your mourning is over, you will find a new mate among the Ssedez."

I glance at the other Ssedez nearby, who are politely pretending not to hear the conversation. Though they're all likely listening in.

The Ssedez are a cohesive species. We are all one family. They have likely been praying during the hundred years since Tiortan died for me to find love again, once my grieving period has passed.

Pvotton shouts, "Gahnin!" He points toward the sky. An enormous shadow, above the clouds, has shrouded the sun.

"The *Hades*," I murmur. As if the name weren't ominous enough, Assura's shock and terror at seeing the ship's outline is. She is not one scared easily. By her face, I can surmise that the ship brings with it all the evil we fear most from the Ten Systems.

One of the Fellamana shouts their word for, "Go!" They each grab the enormous packs they brought with them from town and dash from the jungle toward the human camp.

I grab one by the arm as she passes. "What are you doing?"

"You'll see," she says with a smile and runs after the others, faster than any of my warriors can run.

"How did we miss that they can move so fast?" Pvotton asks.

"I do not know. But we're going to find out what they're doing."

We chase after them, all the Ssedez. The human blasters cannot hurt us. We stayed in the jungle only to keep from causing panic among them. They do not trust us yet, even if their General Nemona mated our commander. The last time most of them saw a Ssedez was when we attacked their ship.

The time for polite diplomacy is over. The Ten Systems is here.

The Fellamana spread out. One stops at the corner of the camp and starts to unload his pack. The others continue to circle the outskirts of the camp.

I grasp another Fellamana by the shoulder. "Tell me what's going on. Now."

He doesn't look up from a glass globe he pulls from his pack. Inside, it is a glowing static burst of blue and red lasers.

"What is that?" Pvotton demands.

"We don't have time," the Fellamana snaps. "Get

everyone inside the camp. Anyone outside it when we turn on the shield will be lost."

"Shield?"

"Yes!" He pushes us toward the camp. "Now quit distracting me." He stands and whistles a high-pitched melody that echoes through the field.

It's answered by one Fellamana a distance away, and then another.

"Come on," I say to Pvotton. "Whatever they're doing, we cannot help." Finding Assura is the best directive now.

My warriors follow me into the camp. The humans are distracted, staring at the sky, their faces touched with horror. The shape of the *Hades* above the cloud cover is becoming clearer, bigger, closer.

Someone shouts, "Battle ready!" The words are relayed across the camp, and the humans spring into action. Among their voices, I hear Assura's. I have become so attuned to hers. I turn toward the sound, dodging around humans disappearing into their shelters and reappearing dressed in armor and carrying weapons.

Those will be useful only if the *Hades* actually lands and doesn't decide to destroy us from the air.

I see her, her hair shining in the sun, her body hugged by the white suit from the Fellamana, a sharp contrast to the humans in their gray uniforms or black shellskin armor.

"Assura!" I call out.

She turns and recognizes me. With a motion for her friends to follow, she runs to meet me.

The words rush out of me as soon as she's near. "The Fellamana say they have—"

"Koviye says they're setting up—"

He appears between us. "Just wait. It'll be fine."

Assura and I glance at the sky. Only the barest hint of clouds protect us from the Ten Systems ship.

"The waiting is over, Koviye," I say, loud enough over the noise of the humans arming themselves. The Ssedez are at my back, all of us strapped with knife holsters across our chests in case hand-to-hand combat is necessary. "If you have something planned, now's the time."

"Jenie." He turns to the woman standing beside Assura. She's striking, with light brown hair swept up onto her head, proud features, and a bearing that is so determined, she must be their acting leader while General Nemona is away.

"Is everyone inside the camp?" Koviye asks her.

A stripe of worry crosses her face. She glances at Assura. "I don't think the scavenging group has returned from the *Origin* wreckage." She looks at the sky. "But there is no time."

"Can we still exit once the shields are up?" Assura asks Koviye.

"Yes, but reentering will be a risk for all of us." His face is grave.

"The shield isn't big enough to cover the wreckage of the *Origin*?" Jenie asks Koviye.

"I'm sorry. It's only big enough for the camp."

Assura exchanges a look with Jenie. "I will go after the ones at the wreckage."

Jenie inhales to protest, but Assura gives a stern shake of her head. "Don't fight me. It's best."

Jenie inhales deeply and nods to Koviye. "Set the shields."

Koviye whistles the open-ended melody the other Fellamana used, then finishes with an extra vibrant tone.

A low hum sounds all around us. Everyone looks up to see where it's coming from, and a silvery sheen covers us. A dome forms in the sky above our heads. We can see through it, but it's as though looking at the sky through water.

"Is it soundproof?" I ask, in awe.

"It makes everything within it undetectable," Koviye says. "Not by sound or sight. To anyone around us, we are now invisible."

"What about from the air?" I press.

"We're untraceable from any direction."

"You're certain the Ten Systems technology and weapons won't penetrate it?" Assura asks.

Koviye turns toward her. "They didn't detect our still-functioning satellite. If they had, they would've destroyed it. The weapons we don't know for sure yet, but the shield has been engineered to withstand what Ten Systems weapons we know of."

There's a chance this may work.

"Still, we must be ready." Jenie turns to her lieutenants. "All soldiers armored and armed form a perimeter inside the dome."

They exit to execute her order.

Jenie grasps Assura's face in her hands. "Be safe." She presses a delicate kiss to Assura's lips. "Come back to me."

A stun shakes down my limbs. It's such an intimate moment. There's obviously love between them. It sends a shock through my chest. My heart feels like it's been locked in a vise.

Assura caresses Jenie's cheek in return. "I always do."

It hurts, watching the closeness between them.

I expected Assura had a lover among her humans, yes, but not a mate. I never thought to ask, and now, because of me, because of the *desidre*, the damn Fellamana Sex Games, and my own unwelcome lust, Assura has been unfaithful.

I have been so preoccupied with my own betrayal of my mourning, I did not think about her relationship attachments. Her heart belongs to another.

I force myself to breathe past the ache in my chest. I must keep my head clear of these inconvenient emotions. We have work to do. "The Ssedez will accompany you." It is a gesture of goodwill to seek amends for causing the *Origin's* crash in the first place.

Jenie gives me a brutal glare. "You are still enemies in my eyes."

Assura turns to me. "Which is why coming with me is a good idea."

That she can look at me at all in front of Jenie speaks to her fortitude and professionalism. I only hope my expression is as stoic. I am not supposed to care about her or her relationships. But I do. Knowing she has a mate is one more reason to never touch her again.

Chapter Fifteen

ASSURA

The look on Gahnin's face is...pale? Can gold be pale?

It reveals some sort of shock. And I have no idea why. So I ignore it.

Koviye gives me a glass device that fits in the palm of my hand. "Stand outside the shield with this, and you'll be able to get back inside. But be careful; we'll all be vulnerable at the moment you reenter."

"We will. Let's go." I turn and jog toward the camp's weapons shelter. There, I stock up on extra blasters, explosives, and knives, collecting enough to supply the soldiers down at the *Origin* wreckage. We have no idea how many weapons they took with them.

I'm glad Gahnin volunteered the Ssedez. It's almost like he read my thoughts. It's the perfect opportunity for him to prove to Jenie, and me, that the Ssedez can be trusted to fight with us.

I spread the weapons among the Ssedez, and we walk

through the Fellamana shield. A strange, cold sensation flows over my skin, followed by a loud pop.

On the other side, Gahnin asks me, "Do you know where the wreckage is?"

"I don't think it's hard to find." I move around to the edge of the camp, and…yeah, I was right.

It doesn't matter how vital our mission. The surreality of the sight takes our breath away.

"We saw it from the air but…" Gahnin's awe matches mine.

The *Origin* sits grounded in the valley, thousands of the jungle's massive trees downed in its path. The devastation to the forest alone is catastrophic. The soil and rock are gouged and reshaped by the impact of the bow as though it were sand.

But the *Origin* is in one piece.

"Do you think she's repairable?" Gahnin asks.

"She has to be. She's all we have." I find a trail in the hillside that's formed from the trips to and from the crash site.

Gahnin grasps my arm and turns me around. "Look."

Behind us, it's as though the camp isn't there. Never was there. As though the entire field is nonexistent.

"It's like the shield warps space, folds it as though it isn't there, unless you're inside it," I say in wonder.

"Fascinating." Gahnin holds up the little rectangular piece of glass Koviye gave us as we left. "Hopefully, this will get us back in as he says."

"It better."

We head to the trail, but then we hear it. The loud boom of a spacecraft, one big enough to fell whole cities, entering the atmosphere. The *Hades*, gleaming obsidian in the flashing sun, blocks out every cloud in the sky.

This is it.

We may as well stand and watch.

Dargule will either fire from the ship, blowing us all to smithereens, or land, planning to capture and torture us all—or just me.

A weapons door on the underside of the ship opens, and I inhale sharply. A laser cannon, capable of incinerating our entire camp, lowers and points directly at us.

This is it.

I reach for Gahnin's hand beside me. He returns my grip with fierce pressure and looks at me with something unfathomable in his eyes.

"I'm sorry," he says. "About what we did to Jenie."

I'm about to ask him what the hell he's talking about, when the high-pitched whine of the cannon charging splits the air.

But just as I expect it to shoot, as my brain starts to think about what's the last thing I want to do before I die—and the thought of kissing Gahnin one more time doesn't sound so bad—

The cannon point drops straight down and fires at the forest directly below the ship. A mile away from us. In the valley beside the *Origin*.

"Hallelujah!" I cry and watch the *Hades* blast a landing pad for itself into the forest floor. "Come on." I yank Gahnin's hand toward the trees before I let go and take off down the path with the Ssedez following me.

My excitement for a fight with Dargule churns in my gut. My chance to redeem myself and free the prisoners has arrived.

It doesn't take long to find the humans who went to the *Origin* crash site. We stock them with the weapons we brought, and everyone turns back toward camp.

Except me.

Gahnin stops. "Come on. We have to get back."

"You go. I've got things to do." Dargule is here—for me. No matter how well protected everyone is by the Fellamana invisibility shield, the *Hades* won't leave until Dargule gets the revenge he wants.

Me going to him, finishing him off before he can wreak any more damage on this planet than he already has, is the best plan. Besides, the *Hades* is where my true rescue mission lies.

I don't need anyone's help to play the spy and assassin. That's what I do best.

I put the glass shield opener into Gahnin's hand. "Go."

Gahnin's brows lower and narrow. "Where are you going?"

"To solve the problem. Tell Jenie I'll return soon. It won't take long."

"No, I will not," he snaps. "Pvotton!" He calls to his warriors heading up the hill.

Pvotton stops and looks back. "Commander?"

"I'm going with Assura to inspect the *Hades*. Tell General Jenie we will return soon."

"We must go with you," Pvotton says. "Otherwise, we cannot get back inside the shield."

I poke Gahnin in the chest between his knives. "I work alone. That's how I'm trained. You'll ruin everything. Go. Back!"

Gahnin examines me, his eyes searching mine. "You are an assassin."

I cringe. "Among other things." He's too close to the truth for me to deny it. It won't be long before he figures out the rest of my secrets.

He nods and turns to his Ssedez. "Go, Pvotton." He gives the shield opener to him. Pvotton inhales to protest, but

Gahnin talks over him. "That's an order." Pvotton nods and leads the Ssedez and humans back toward the camp.

"Don't be stupid." I shove him. "You won't be able to get back in the camp without the glass device from Koviye."

"Neither will you."

"I'm not going back until Dargule is off this planet."

"Neither am I."

There's nothing I can do. I can't force him to leave. The best I could hope is to somehow lose him. Or, I could insult his honor.

I glare at him. "Are you doing this for some 'save the girl' bullshit?"

He can't meet my eyes. He looks everywhere but me—the ground, the sky, the trees. The loud roar of the *Hades* landing rends the air, but all I see is Gahnin, being awkward.

I start to laugh. "Right. Go back. I'll take care of myself." I turn away.

He grasps my shoulder to stop me. "Assura, I'm coming with you." There's a thick authority in his voice, the kind no one would disobey. Except me.

I face him, astonished. "I'm just another human, remember? I don't matter."

The sincerity on his face is so harsh it's blinding. "I want revenge against the Ten Systems as badly as you do. You cannot take this chance away from me."

Of course. They killed his mate. "Now, that's a reason I can't refuse."

The ground shakes with the impact of the *Hades* landing. I glance back at the ship, now seamless with the forest on the horizon. Dargule is here: my worst enemy, whom I didn't get to kill; my prisoners, whom I never set free.

I get another chance to make this right. And this time, I have to succeed.

If anyone deserves to accompany me on my mission—

Gahnin's right—it's him.

A sinking feeling weighs down my stomach. He's going to find out about the Ssedez Dargule has held captive for a hundred years. There is no doubt I will lose Gahnin when he learns it. But he deserves to know the truth. We have to get inside the ship.

"I'm in charge," I snap. "I know the ship. I know the crew. I know how the Ten Systems operate."

"Agreed."

"I have a strategy. You do as I command. I will not let you jeopardize this mission. People's lives are at stake." I don't say that it's more than the lives of the rebellion; it's the prisoners on board the *Hades*, too.

His expression darkens, and he glares at me as if I've said something insulting. His paleness from before when he saw me with Jenie is gone.

Is that what it was? Me kissing her confused him? Whatever. I don't give a shit. I *can't.*

"I'll watch your back. We're partners," he says stiffly, as though it's the most diplomatic thing he's ever agreed to.

"You can come. But if I tell you to fall back, to leave, you'll do it."

"Not if your safety is compromised. We are a team. You aren't in this alone." I don't want to give in, on principle, but he's right. I don't want to do this by myself.

I hold out my hand. "Humans shake on agreements."

He grabs my hand in a firm grip.

I smile. "Let's get our revenge."

Sneaking up on the *Hades* isn't the hard part. It's getting inside.

We crouch behind a barricade of ashes from the trees

burned by the *Hades*'s laser gun, and we wait. They have to open the ship's door sometime. Gods know how long it will take, though.

"Do you think they know about the *desidre*?" Gahnin says, keeping his voice low.

"Jenie said our medics figured out an antidote from the *Origin*'s medical supplies pretty fast, so my guess is the *Hades* crew has analyzed the atmosphere and made one, too."

"How do you know?"

I shrug, trying to ignore the anxiety I feel at being this close to my old ship. "We'll know if they come out and start dry humping each other."

He raises his brows. "Really? Jokes? Now?"

Better humor than fear. "It's not like you even know how to laugh, so what does it matter?"

His mouth thins into a line. "I know how to laugh."

"Really? When?"

"I…" He pauses, thinking. "I laugh sometimes."

"No, you don't." I'm almost ready to. He's so defensive.

He glares at me. "You have known me four days. Two of which you were unconscious."

"You have no laugh lines."

"Ssedez do not get wrinkles."

Well, that's convenient. "How old are you, anyway?" The Ssedez aboard the Hades when I left it was a prisoner left over from the genocide war a hundred years ago, so he had to have been at least—

"One hundred and twenty-two," he says. "By the Ten Systems measurement."

Gods. I gulp hard. I must have misheard. That can't be right. "How old were you when your mate died?"

Any smile that might have been in his eyes fades. His gaze travels to the sky. "Twenty-two."

My breath stops in my lungs. "You were mated so young."

"Tiortan was only twenty," he muses quietly. "We were practically kids. It's unusual. But when the Attachment happens..." He takes a deep breath. "It's considered good fortune to find one's mate early in life." He says a phrase in Ssedez involving sounds only his dexterous tongue could make.

"Why?"

"When the heart is full, life is fuller."

"Has your heart been empty since she died?" I feel like he needs to open his eyes and live.

But my question has the opposite effect I intend. He closes his eyes, and his face contorts like he's in pain. "Do not ask me that."

"All I meant is—"

"I know what you meant," he seethes through his teeth. If we weren't in hiding, he would've yelled it. "You meant I should move on. Guess what? I fucked you, didn't I? So that must mean I'm over her." He glares at me, and I stare back, unable to believe what he just said.

And then I think about it.

And think about it some more.

Oh my gods, no.

"Does that mean..." My voice shakes. "Please tell me you've had sex with other people since she died."

He leans on his knees and stares off into the forest.

"Someone besides me," I press, needing an answer.

But he doesn't respond. He won't even look at me, and my heartbeat accelerates. It would explain so many things. His fervency. His sex drive. His unquenchable need for more of me. If I hadn't had sex in a hundred years, I'd be the same.

Or, I am the same. With him. Not that that means anything.

So, his unfettered lust has nothing to do with how attracted he is to me. It's because he's been denying himself for a century. But that doesn't explain…

"Why me?" I whisper.

"I do not know." He says it with such finality, the subject is closed. He's not commenting anymore to assuage my curiosity.

Which is good, because a loud clanking comes from beyond us, and the *Hades* hangar bay door opens.

If my heart was racing before, it slows, trudging in my chest like it's just been filled with mud. My hands get clammy, and I realize why I've been so chatty and provoking him with painful questions.

I'm nervous. No matter how strong my sense of duty is that I must do this, I don't want to be here. I escaped and thought I'd never see this ship again or the people on it. But *he* might not even be onboard. Maybe they gave Dargule's ship to someone else.

"Assura, remember to breathe," Gahnin whispers beside me, and I'm suddenly grateful he's here. I don't have to face my fears alone.

I glance back at the ship. It's going to be okay. We have to succeed.

Out walks my worst nightmare.

Chapter Sixteen

GAHNIN

She goes so still beside me, it's like she's not even there.

She makes no sound, no movement. I have to look at her to be sure she has not run away.

It must be a technique, something she does to remain undetectable. But her pallor is paler than I have ever seen her, like all the blood has drained away from her skin. She does not respond when I encourage her again to breathe, so I assume my attention is unwelcome, and stop.

The human standing at the end of the ship's gangplank looks like someone straight from the old videos of the Ten Systems genocide war against the Ssedez.

I was not old enough to be a warrior until I turned thirty, after the war was over, despite my mate being among the dead. The Ssedez hid themselves on an unknown planet, so the Ten Systems would never find us again—and they have not, until now. But I have seen images of the conflict, and their soldiers looked just like this.

The soldier in black armor and helmet stands surveying the forest. He must be this Dargule who Assura fears. There's no curiosity in his stance or gesture. No wondering or searching for discovery. Nothing but cold, hard supremacy. Like he expects everything, even the dirt, to bow down beneath his feet.

His head and shoulders square forward, posture rigid and domineering. If he pulled blasters and started shooting at the trees for not bending before him, it would not surprise me.

"Is it him?" I whisper to Assura. "Is the one in the front Dargule?"

She gulps hard, her neck clenching, then she turns her eyes to me. Sheer terror. She looks frightened enough to run.

I grasp her hand. "We do not have to do this. We can go back. You do not have to be the hero."

She squeezes my hand as though agreeing with me, then shakes her head and looks back at Dargule. "Looks like he took the antidote."

I want to laugh, and I would, if she were not so obviously terrified.

I glance at her again, and she has a blaster in her hand. I did not even hear her take it out. She hands it to me silently.

I examine the black, short-range weapon with titanium settings and nuclear charger. "These are useless against their armor."

"It works if you aim for the joint separations." She settles her own blaster's aim on the top of the bunker of ashes. "Dargule will take his helmet off. Fire on him when he does. Don't bother with anyone else until he is down."

A dozen Ten Systems soldiers march down the plank, their matching black armor clanking in unison.

"How do you know he'll take his helmet off?" I ask.

"Because he will. He believes he's invincible—his greatest weakness." Her tone is as frigid as snows in winter.

The twelve soldiers disappear into the woods, and another twelve march out.

But my eyes are only for Dargule, who, true to what Assura said, reaches for his helmet, takes it off, and we fire—

At the same moment, an armored lieutenant steps in front of Dargule. Both our laser blasts glance off his helmet.

"Shit." Assura ducks behind the bank of ashes, and so do I.

Shouts sound behind us. Blaster shots explode in the bunker protecting us.

"What's our escape plan?" I yell over the noise of the blasters.

"There's an escape plan?"

"You said you had a strategy!" I snap, wishing now I had asked more questions.

"I do. Kill Dargule." I notice her hands are shaking. She is not okay. Something is wrong.

I have to help her focus. "There'll be a dozen soldiers on us in thirty seconds. Do we fight them or try to hide in the forest?"

She looks at me, and there's steel in her eyes. The kind of courage that comes only when facing great fear. "I have to get on board the *Hades*. It's not enough to kill Dargule. We can't let the Ten Systems find out about the Fellamana. They'll destroy them."

"Agreed."

"We can't let the Ten Systems find out the Ssedez are still alive, either." She shoves her blaster at me. "You need to run."

"No. I will not."

"You promised you'd fall back if I told you to." She starts to fumble with her weapons.

"But not like this. You need help, Assura. You are shaking." I clasp her impotent hands that are struggling and failing to undo her weapons belt. "What are you doing?"

"I'm going to surrender."

I grab her arm to stop her. "No."

"You never should've come!" The fear quaking her voice has not lessened; if anything, it's increased to include me. "You Ssedez destroyed your home world so the Ten Systems would never find out your species survived. If they see you, it'll be for nothing!"

"I am one lone Ssedez. My presence here does not give away my entire species." A laser blast hits the barricade of ashes next to my head. "Their weapons will not hurt me. There's a chance I could fight through them. Even if I cannot, the worst that would happen is they restrain me. You have no natural armor. They could kill you."

Her eyes widen. She knows I am right.

I point toward the trees. "Hide. You may be able to sneak aboard the ship while I draw their fire." And it will allow her time to gather courage over her fear.

She stares at the jungle, her eyes darting from tree to tree, plotting a course to the ship. "It could work."

"Go," I say, and she scrambles off low in the bushes. Too soon, I lose sight of her. I watched her sneak into the forest, and now I can't see her, her movements too calculated to be detected among the trees.

I smile, my respect for her skills mounting. *Damn, she's good.*

It is my turn. I stand and face the fire.

A dozen blast shots hit me in the chest.

Chapter Seventeen

ASSURA

Once I'm concealed by the foliage, I turn back to watch.

The armed soldiers encroach on Gahnin, and he takes their firepower like it's mere water beating against his chest. He walks around the barricade toward them, shooting from his blaster. His aim is not as good as mine, but two soldiers go down as he hits two shots in the kinks of their neck armor.

I move from tree to tree, keeping my eyes on Gahnin. He is impressive, fearsome, even terrifying. And it's so damn hot. I have to not think about it to continue moving. I want to stand and watch. He takes out the soldiers one by one.

He shoves one to the ground with a hand. The soldier lands so hard, even with the armor, he goes unconscious. One tries to fight back, but Gahnin pulls a knife from his chest holster and stabs the soldier in the shoulder crease of his armor on the first swipe.

They fall like flimsy dolls, victim to his inhuman strength. I never put together just how dangerously lethal he is. But he doesn't kill any of them, merely removes them from his path, and incapacitates them so they can't attack him again from behind.

I dodge to the next set of trees, crouching closer and closer to the shadow of the *Hades*.

The soldiers start to retreat in fear until Gahnin comes face to face with Dargule. Gahnin lifts the blaster, aiming for Dargule's head. I hold my breath, desperate to see the end of the vile monster who's fueled my nightmares.

Dargule's face, though, rather than afraid, looks gleeful.

He grabs something from his weapons belt. Before I have to time to wonder what it is, warn Gahnin, or do something about it, he points it at Gahnin and shoots.

Gahnin doesn't even duck, assuming it's just another blaster that won't harm him. What erupts from Dargule's weapon is not the green light of a blaster's laser. It's white static, so hot I feel the blast of heat radiate to where I'm hidden, several meters away.

It hits Gahnin, and he starts to shake as though in a seizure, and static sparks come off his body. He falls to his knees.

I freeze in horror, disbelieving what I'm seeing. But Dargule bends down to shock Gahnin again, and my heart screams through my throat.

"No!" I run from the trees, holding down the trigger of my blaster, aiming rapid fire at Dargule's head.

But it's as though he predicted my movement. He points his weapons at me.

The white-hot charges seem to latch onto my blast shots, disintegrating them. One connects with my blaster and heats the weapon until it's so hot, I'm forced to drop it or burn my hands.

Dargule shouts, "Seize her!" And every soldier who hid from Gahnin and remains conscious comes at me.

If it were three or even four of them, I could fight them off. But seven is too many for even me. Rather than risk injury to myself—knowing if I'm knocked out, I'll have zero chance of helping Gahnin—I put my hands in the air in surrender.

Two of the soldiers, who I recognize by their uniform rankings, grab my arms and restrain them behind my back. Their holds are inferior, and I could break them with a twist of my torso, but breaking free now is counterproductive.

I arch my neck around them to see Gahnin, prostrate on the ground, but I breathe a sigh of relief. He is moving, writhing and moaning in pain, but conscious.

The soldiers walk me forward, and my gaze locks with Dargule's.

My shoulders start to shake. His eyes probably used to be dark brown, but whether it's genetic alteration or just corruption from his years of cruelty, they're black now. It looks like he has no irises.

He didn't used to scare me. Or I was so habitually guarding myself against my fear of him, I lived with mental defenses like armor inside my head. But in the time that I've been separated from him, in my six weeks of freedom, I've grown soft.

I've let those defenses down.

"Stop," he orders.

I am taller than he is. So at least I have that to my advantage. That and nothing else. That's why he stops me so far away from him, so the height difference isn't obvious.

Dargule's dark eyes shine from his pale face with calculated malice. I know that look. He's already planning what twisted things he'll do to me and Gahnin, and it contorts my stomach so hard, I have the urge to vomit.

A creepy smile stretches his face. "Assur. What a pleasure." His gaze darts to Gahnin on the ground. "Tell me, who is your Ssedez friend?"

I barely suppress my shiver of disgust as the sound slithers down my spine. His voice, with his helmet off and free of the scrambler, is low, but in the opposite way of Gahnin's resonant tone. It's like Dargule's is vacant somehow. Vacant of the things that make a person human—normal emotions beyond his capability. My days with the Ssedez and Fellamana are proof: "humanity," or the respect for all living beings, is something missing more often from humans than other species, at least, in my experience so far.

But I force myself to get over my reaction to him and respond to what he said. Assur isn't my name anymore. "Who's Assur?" I say, low enough it's almost a whisper.

By instinct, he comes closer so he can hear me. Which is what I wanted—for him to feel threatened by our height difference. Though perhaps that's stupid. The more threatened he is, the crueler he has the potential to be.

He tilts his head in a gesture having nothing to do with curiosity—more like sociopathy. "Is this a game? Or are you in an identity crisis, my little tormentor?"

The nickname slugs me with a punch of revulsion. He used to say it when I was most at his mercy, when there was nothing I could do to disobey him without landing myself in a torture chamber or worse, losing my job as his right hand and leaving the prisoners to face a true psychopath instead. There is nothing *little* about me, but he said it to screw with me and make me feel small, part of his vile manipulations. His ability to see what will torment people most and remind them of it as often as possible is insanity-inducing.

Him calling me that helps me retrieve my former mental armor. I have to protect myself and not give in to my fear if I hope to survive this.

Still on the ground, still curled in pain, Gahnin speaks in a hoarse voice. "Are you some *little* version of authority we're supposed to be afraid of? Where's your commanding officer?"

Brilliant. Even in his weakened state, Gahnin's already caught on to Dargule's game. His is a voice sent from someplace nearest to heaven as I've ever heard.

I have a partner. I'm not alone in this. Not like I used to be.

Dargule's expression ices over. Oh shit. That ruthless, emotionless gaze that is his natural state is the one that makes me sweat most. It means he's going to drop the civilized act and shoot straight for pain.

He lasers a look at me. "You stole my prototype." The weapon I took from him was his latest *toy*, as he calls his torture devices, though he has a new one now that's better. He had worked on the old one for months. I destroyed it before I left with the *Origin*. It was the only way I knew I'd get past him to free the prisoners, if he was without that weapon. The rest of my plan didn't work.

Dargule's mouth twists in a vicious grin that on him is terrifying. "But you're mine now." He points his shock gun, or whatever the hell is in his hand, at me. "Back away from her," he orders to the guards.

They let me go. I have no way of protecting myself. I hold my breath, assuming he's going to shock me the same way he did Gahnin.

A silver stream of static pours from his weapon and forms into standing bars in front of me. Blindingly bright lines form in front of my face. I don't touch them, sure they'll do to me what they did to Gahnin—worse.

I try to go around them but can't. I turn, and they're all around me, above me. An electromagnetic cage. Beneath me, a solid floor forms, made of—I don't know what. The whole cage emits a high-pitched hum.

Beside me inside the cage, Gahnin groans on the ground and rolls to his side, clutching his chest. At least he's not dead.

"Oh, goodie," Dargule chimes gleefully, outside the cage, next to my face. "I love it when my new toys work better than I expected."

I have no idea what the hell that thing is he used on us, or how it could possibly work on Gahnin when no other weapon other than fire could. But this is bad. Very bad.

This is a cage I have no idea how to escape from.

I glare at Dargule and his expression of sick pleasure. "What is that thing?" He'll most likely take the excuse to brag about it. Learning more about the device is my best hope.

"It's an electroshock gun, powered by a mini-hadron collider," he says with a breathy tone that on anyone else I would associate with ecstasy. Which, I guess for him, this is.

"A hadron collider? With gold atoms?" So it creates heat—like hotter than a supernova. That's why it worked on Gahnin. If he can be harmed with fire, then superheated blasts, hotter than fire, would definitely work, too.

I glance at Gahnin still curled in on himself with pain. A sinking sensation slams my innards. What if it singed his nervous system, all the way to his brain?

I try to spit at Dargule through the bars of the cage. But my saliva sizzles in the static between the bars.

Dargule's smile of vile pleasure widens. "This is so perfect, I couldn't have scripted it."

I sneer at him. "You know how the script ends, right?"

He hums lightly. "With you catatonic and kept alive for the pure purpose of experiencing pain. To test new torture devices, of course."

I inhale hard and let a vindictive smile show. "It ends with you begging us not to kill you."

"Oh sweet Assur," he says with a stilting stop to the word sweet, like he doesn't know its true meaning. "By tomorrow, you'll be so far gone with fever from the toxin on this planet, you won't even remember your own name."

Part of his plan is apparently to deprive us of the antidote to the planet's atmosphere. I grit my teeth. I will find a way to escape before that happens.

"It's perfect, really." Dargule sighs, looking around at the trees. "They tell me they're not sure what effect the fever will have on the human body, so we need test subjects. And here you are."

He doesn't know that he'd be sexually torturing us. He'll be surprised, then.

"No antidote will work completely," I warn. "You won't last a day on this planet even with it." He's not someone who goes for sexual things. He seems to have a hard-on only for pain. So when the *desidre* starts to affect him, he's not going to be able to satisfy it.

With luck, it'll motivate him to leave the planet.

He clicks his tongue in the negative. "That's because your pathetic crew and the *Origin's* out-of-date tech didn't give you the antidote we have."

I scowl. That's entirely possible.

He taps his fingers impatiently. "Now, as fun as this tête-à-tête is, I have to find the rest of your rebel crew. But do not fret, dear. I will return."

My lip curls in disgust, and I have the urge to provoke him into revealing more to me—his motives, his strategies. He loves to brag.

But I need to help Gahnin more.

Dargule turns his back, and I slide to my knees beside Gahnin.

I brush his cheek. "Gahnin?" I whisper, not wanting anyone to hear me.

His eyes crack open, and for a moment, he just stares at me.

There's something in his gaze that reaches inside my chest, wraps around my heart, and makes me feel both stronger and more afraid at the same time.

He reaches up to put his hand over mine.

"Are you okay?" I ask.

He croaks, his voice tight. "Just a bit of pain." His body quakes, like with an aftershock.

I'm worried, but at least he's able to move his arm and speak. But I decide humor is better. "Wimp."

He chuckles, then winces. "Correct."

Chapter Eighteen

GAHNIN

It takes me a few hours, but the pain eventually subsides enough, I am able to sit up.

Assura relays everything Dargule said.

Four guards are posted around us, each at one corner of our electromagnetic prison—or whatever it is made of.

The guards are far enough away that we are able to talk quietly enough so they cannot hear us. It's a lapse in judgment that they are not spying on what we're saying, or perhaps a sign of just how cocky Dargule is about the quality of his trap.

Which turns out to be justified.

We try pieces of items we have on us to deflect the static of the bars. All our efforts get us is a burned hole in my boot and an incinerated button from her suit. We inspect the floor, guessing it must be made of the same energy, though it feels different—in addition to the obvious fact that it doesn't cause us to pass out from pain—more solid somehow. There are no cracks or weaknesses.

By the middle of the night, we're forced to admit, we're fucked.

And by the time the sun comes up, the *topuy* will wear off, and we will be vulnerable to the *desidre*. With zero privacy. With our worst enemies watching.

We sit side by side looking up, through the cage bars, into the night sky at the planet's moons heading toward the horizon. The light from our static cage bars casts striped lines across our faces.

"We need a strategy," she says.

"I have zero ideas." I'm depleted actually. Physically, I feel awful. But that's not what bothers me. It's how this circumstance is going to affect Assura, with us being trapped alone again with nothing but the *desidre* for company. I do not want this for her, or me. More chemically induced sex is not how I wanted our relationship to go.

Not that it is a "relationship" or anything resembling it, but I cannot stop my brain from dwelling on her.

She does not seem bothered, though. She's all planning. "When I was in the jungle, the worst time of day for the *desidre* was midafternoon, when the sun was hottest."

"Not sure how that's helpful."

"I found that if I avoided giving myself an orgasm all morning while it was less awful, then by afternoon, I was delirious with the fever."

"Wait. There were times when it was worse than others?" I groan. "I thought it was just all misery all the time."

"Well." She sighs heavily. "It did make orgasms feel like…well…almost as good as yours."

That makes me smile for the first time in hours. I cannot decide if it's good that she does not glance my way to see. It makes me remember the other awful part about this situation. "There has to be a way we can satisfy it without having to have actual intercourse." Not that that makes the other stuff any less problematic for her, but somehow, it seems less deceitful.

She stiffens. "Why? Feeling shy now?" There's a bitter tinge to her voice.

"No, it…" I scrub a hand through my hair. "We've already forced you to be unfaithful enough. It breaks my heart for you to have to do it again." If my mate had cheated on me the way Assura has cheated on Jenie with me…I would have been in danger of doing extreme violence.

And I'm not sure, if Jenie tried, whether I would feel right about defending myself.

A sour taste brims in my mouth, and my stomach knots like it's been filled with acid.

Mating bonds are so sacred to the Ssedez. Being unfaithful is biologically impossible for the males and so rare for the females, I know no one who's ever done it. I have only heard stories.

"Unfaithful to what? My hand?" She laughs.

My heart trips over itself. Surely, she cannot be so without feeling. "To Jenie," I whisper, shocked.

She turns to face me, her expression half in shadow, but the glow from our prison lets me see she's surprised. "Jenie?"

I have to swallow hard to say it. "You are in love, yes? Mated? Or soon will be?"

Her expression softens, and she grasps my hand. "Oh, my Ssedez. It was what we call a casual relationship."

"Casual?" I have misunderstood and betrayed my concern for her. I am not supposed to care about anything concerning her—and I am failing.

My vulnerability grips at my anger and pulls at my chest. I do not understand this woman or these humans or any human. "What is casual about love? There is nothing more powerful in the universe." I have lived with the grief of losing it for ten decades. I am both marked and scarred forever.

She leans her head on her knee, and her expression is full

of sensitivity and patience. "I love her for the extraordinary woman she is. She is glorious to share a bed with. But I never had any desire to be exclusive with her or to have a commitment from her."

This translates into nothing I have experienced before. I have seen other unmated Ssedez warriors engage in such relationships. But I have never succeeded. "So, you have not cheated or been unfaithful with me?"

She grasps my hand. "No. I'm free to sleep with whoever and whenever I like." She says it with lightness almost like it is a joke.

But there is nothing funny about it to me. "That means that what you and I have is also…"— I have to swallow before I can say it—"…casual." The acid eating at my stomach, rather than lessening, gets worse. It starts to burn in my gut. There is nothing casual about the Attachment that is still brewing inside me for her. It is a force of nature, one that I can try to deny or avoid. One that I must conquer.

She hesitates but eventually agrees. "Yes, this is casual."

I stare off in the forest. "It is also chemically induced."

"What do you mean?"

"We have been lovers only because of the *desidre*." I say this because I need it to be true. That is the only reason I still crave her body like an addiction.

She stops breathing, so I have to look at her. "That… is…" She stutters with confusion, and her voice morphs to indignation. "Do you honestly believe that? You think the only reason we're like this"—she gestures back and forth between us—"like a damn lit fuse waiting to go off, is because of the *desidre*?"

"Of course it is," I assert but cannot stop from noticing how her breasts are propped up against her knees, from remembering what they felt like in my hands.

She tosses her head back and stares at the stars. "You

know, they say it's the *desidre*, but I haven't felt like having sex with anyone but you, and the Fellamana told me the *desidre* should make us want to have it with anyone who breathes. Why is that?"

My breath stops, and I do not want to answer. "I do not know. I have never indulged in casual sex." It would have been disrespectful to Tiortan's memory. Still is.

She drags her gaze down to mine, and there's a mischievous glint to her eye, like she knows something. "You are what we call a serial monogamist, Gahnin. You need to wrap your logic around sex as recreation, not only something to indulge in when one is mated or committed or whatever."

I try; I do. But it's as though my brain is a computer and the entry code is wrong. Like my instincts do not acknowledge this concept as possible. There is no reason I can think of for sex unless it is because I want her to be *mine*.

"Besides." Her voice lowers and thickens. "There was no *desidre* or pressure from the Fellamana that last time. We'd more than satisfied the *desidre* during the games. We didn't have the toxin for an excuse then."

Oh Gods. "In the hallway…against the wall…" I have to close my eyes to keep from reaching for her. It's like I'm there again, driving inside her so hard, even her tight ass shakes from my hips slapping against her.

"When you forced me to beg before you would fuck me." Her tone sounds rasping, so full of sex, if I was not already getting hard, I'm now stone.

My mouth is open, my breath coming fast. She makes me want her again with the full of my yearning to bury myself inside her. It's always there, simmering beneath the surface, even in our most life-threatening moments.

She uncovers it, so I have to clench my fists to keep from grabbing her and pulling her beneath me.

I stare up at the stars, too. "Do you know what you do to

me?"

"I want to know." Her hand graces my chin and urges me to look at her. "Without me having to beg."

Her mouth is right there, in front of my eyes. I stare at it, and she parts her lips. Her lush human tongue licks across her lower lip, and I remember how those lips felt wrapped around my cock. And how she looked with my silver come dripping down her chin.

She leans forward and kisses me.

It's like the answer to every prayer I have had since I met her. She wants me. Her mouth sucks on my lips and pulls on my tongue like she'd devour me if she could. Her plump lips are full between my teeth as I nibble across them—grateful I have been able to keep my fangs from descending so I may have the pleasure of her mouth on mine.

She climbs over me and straddles my hips. She's high on her knees, her head above me, her hands cupping my face.

I cling to her back, run my hands down her torso, and sink my fingers into her ass. Damn, I wish we had no audience, so I could get her naked.

Even in the faint light, the guards can see us.

She lowers her knees and brushes the apex of her thighs against my hardness through my leather.

I groan and hold her against me. "Like that. Harder."

She obliges, grinding her hips into me, sliding her hot cunt up and down the hardened length of me until I'm hopelessly, helplessly grinding back.

"Beg me," she whispers against my mouth.

I growl through my teeth. "If there were no guards, I'd have you on your back and naked already."

She lifts her mouth and stares in my eyes. "That's not begging."

I have to think about it, and I wonder if she's serious. If I beg, would she have sex here and now anyway, despite our audience? Do I want her to?

Gods, yes.

It's surprising to discover, I do not care who sees us, only that I get inside her. "Please, let me fuck you."

She sinks her teeth into my lip and clamps down hard. I flinch but moan at the same time. She can bite me anywhere, as hard as she wants. A craving sprouts in me for it.

I snake my thumb inside her mouth and stroke her little teeth. "Bite me."

She holds my hand away from her mouth. "Not unless you beg."

My brain stutters. My instinct is to order her to do it, to feed her imperatives like I want to feed her my cock. But I force my thoughts to work backward. "I need you to bite me. I need to feel your teeth on my skin."

She strokes my thumb along her lip, deliberately still, denying me her bite.

I cannot take the games. The longing in me is like the need for a volcano to erupt. Except I need her to do it. "Please, Assura. I'm begging." My words are oozing desperation, but I do not care.

"Good boy," she croons, and bites down on my thumb, sending pleasure searing through my veins.

Chapter Nineteen

ASSURA

I bite him so hard, on human skin, I'd taste blood.

But not on him. His cock hardens between my thighs; it jerks and throbs against my clit, even through our clothes.

I drag my teeth down the length of his thumb with excruciating slowness, and his breath echoes in fast, shallow drops against my neck. He likes this. A lot.

And so do I. I do it to each of his fingers, then bite his palm so hard, he groans loud and low.

I cover his mouth with my hand. "Shh. Don't make a sound."

"If you say so," he whispers against my palm, and his obedience is delectable.

I wish I had a knife with me. "Do you want me to dig my claws into your chest?"

"*Gods*, please." He's begging for real now, without me making him.

I can't help my mischievous smile. I like it. I want him

begging me for it, almost as much as I want him thrusting inside me, pounding me to mind-bending orgasm.

I sink my nails into his pectorals with as much force as my arms can bear. My biceps are shaking with the tightening of my muscles, and I grit my teeth. My fingers sink into his flesh. He rocks against me. His sighs are ragged. If we weren't surrounded by guards, they'd be low cries and moans of pleasure.

He grasps my forearms and presses my nails in even deeper. Then, with the force of our combined strength, I drag them down his chest.

He gasps so hard, he stops breathing, and I fear he's going to come.

The sensation of scraping my nails across him, taking the full force of my strength out on him, is blissful. I grind my hips against him, the pleasure mounting in me, too.

But I don't want us to orgasm, not until he's inside me.

I loose his hands from my arms and push him onto his back. I lean over his face. "Do you want me to fuck you?"

"Yessss." His Ssedez tongue hisses around the *S* like the gold serpents his kind are descended from.

I wish I could get naked, but with no desire to give the guards more of a show than we already are, I merely unbutton the fuck panel in my suit and send up a prayer of thanks to the Fellamana and their prurient, yet practical, clothing styles.

His fingers shaking, he yanks open his leather fly and pulls out his cock, and I'm grateful it appears the Ssedez are always commando. Or, at least, this one is.

He holds himself at the angle I need, and I lower my hips over him.

The tip of him notches inside me, and as I sink down, I burrow my nails into his chest again. It's good. Excruciating, tortuously good. He stretches me to the brink, fills me up, and reaches so far inside me, I have to lean forward at an angle for our hips to meet.

The base of his cock rubs against my clit, and I can't hold still.

I fuck him, shamelessly. I don't give a shit who's watching. Dargule himself could be standing outside the cage, staring at me, and I wouldn't stop or slow.

I lift my pelvis up and down in a rhythm so fast, my thighs burn. But it's delicious. The glide of him both inside me and against my clit—he's a dual torture device made for killing me with orgasms.

The first climax hits me so fiercely, I fall onto his chest, but I can't stop. I don't want to stop. I slide over him back and forth, not slowing my rhythm.

His neck, his throat, is next to my mouth, his body hard beneath mine, quaking with the thrill of building ecstasy.

His pulse beats against my mouth, and the temptation to bite him is irresistible. I latch onto his throbbing vein with my teeth.

It sets off his orgasm, and I cover his mouth to stifle his climactic shout, though he's impossible to silence.

I bite harder, as strong as my jaw can. He holds my head to him, like he only wants more, for my teeth to go impossibly deeper into him. I enjoy it—the power, the influence, the ability to set him off by giving in to my urge to cause pain. It's freeing. It's…

Something cuts through my blissful haze. A sound. Almost like…clapping.

I lift my head, and there he is, his obsidian eyes glittering in the light of the static cage bars.

"Brava," Dargule says to me, a sadistic smile stretching his face.

I'm so shocked, I freeze. I know I thought I wouldn't care if he was watching. But, now I see him, I feel violated. Like I've exposed a piece of my deepest, most valuable part of myself to *him*.

He is worse than my worst enemy. He has been my torturer. My jailor. My master. My...

"I like your new form of torture," he soothes. "I'd never thought of it. Though I don't know why. I'll bet it makes him tell you his darkest secrets." He rubs his hands together like this is something delicious.

He hums, thinking. "Now that I know how much you like it, I'll make you do it to all of them. Would you like that?"

A sick feeling percolates in my stomach. The urge to vomit is so eruptive, I slide off Gahnin onto the floor.

But I don't take my eyes off Dargule; that would be a fatal mistake.

He lowers his voice like he's whispering an intimate secret. "There are thirty prisoners aboard the Hades right now. How long do you think it would take you to fuck all of them?"

Sweat sprouts all over my body. I'm incapable of saying anything. If I open my mouth, the only thing that will come out is the contents of my stomach.

"Breathe," Gahnin whispers to me. "I would never let him do that to you."

It gives me small comfort. I know how Dargule's mind works. He's seen my attachment to Gahnin now. A fatal, *stupid* mistake. If Dargule threatened to set Gahnin aflame, which he would, I'd have no choice but to do anything he said.

Including have sex with every prisoner on that ship. And likely the crew as well.

But he's not done. Dargule loves his mind torture, and once he sees he's hit a mark, it encourages him. I reach inside myself, desperately searching for my mental defenses. I have to hide my reaction from him. Weakness will cost me everything.

"Tell me something, Assur," he murmurs softly, like

a lover to an intimate friend. "Which did you like better? Fucking him? Or hurting him?"

I gasp, and my breath gets stuck inside my lungs.

"Oh, my little torturer." He lifts his fingers as though to touch me through the bars of the cage if he could. "Don't try to deny it. You will always like inflicting pain first. You're a sadist by nature. Pain is what you do best."

He backs away and leaves, disappearing into the darkness.

I crawl to the edge of the cage.

And vomit.

Chapter Twenty

My whole body vibrates with the need to sever every one of Dargule's limbs. To crush his skull into a thousand pieces and feel his brain squish between my fingers like mud.

And I could do it. If not for this forsaken cage.

If not for the fact that Assura is the one who deserves the pleasure of killing him. I'll settle for the rest of his crew.

Assura is on her hands and knees, her body wracked by dry heaves.

My heart feels sick to watch her. It physically hurts. I want to comfort her. Though I don't know how or if she'll let me. Or if there really is any comfort to be gotten except for escaping and getting revenge on that perversion of a monster in human form.

I take a deep breath. I can barely think about how magnificent it was to have her riding me, to feel her teeth and nails digging into me as hard as she could. It gave me a satisfaction that sex alone cannot supply. It made me fantasize about what it would be like to have her fangs in me—if she were Ssedez—which I never should've done.

But even the fantasies feel tainted now.

I wonder for how long Dargule was watching us. Did he just walk up and see us orgasm? Did he see our entire lovemaking? Has he been out there for hours in the dark listening to every word we say?

I cannot try to comfort Assura and risk him seeing. It would show more vulnerability in her, in me, in us.

It's too dark to see beyond five feet away from the cage. The lights from the static bars do not go past that.

Dargule could still be watching, out behind the trees.

But I hear a clanging noise from the direction of the ship, and lights from inside are exposed as the plank is lowered. I watch Dargule walk inside, and the door closes behind him.

There are still guards watching us, but *he* will not see.

Assura sits back on her heels and wipes her mouth. Her hands shake, and her breathing is ragged. There's a ravaged look on her face...ravaged by fear...

I go to her and wrap my arms around her. She's stiff at first and almost protests. I cradle her cheek in my hand. "Let me help you," I whisper.

Her eyes fall closed, and she softens in to me, letting me hold her. She rests her head on my shoulder, and her hands cling to my arms. Her chest is rising and falling too fast, her breaths still at panicked speed.

There's a rightness to having her against me. Feeling her, holding her—it fills me. It eases the hole in my chest that I have been living with for too long. Like sunshine after the most frigid of winters or water after years of dry heat, she revitalizes me. A rejection of the feeling grips my stomach. I have not felt this since Tiortan died. And I'm feeling it for this human.

I let go of her, wanting the feeling to go away, and

refocus on my dedication to revenge and to Tiortan, who I'm supposed to mourn for another century. I have to focus on our mission. "We're going to get out of this."

She turns her head side to side, more than a no, like a negation of herself. "It's true," she chokes.

"What's true?"

She hides her face from me. It's so strange. Assura does not hide; she does not show shame. I do not understand what could make her do that.

"What *he* said," she murmurs so low, I almost do not hear.

Oh, she's worried about the other thing he said. "Do not listen to him."

"He's right."

Her words hit me like blaster fire. I think I know what she means. "It used to be your job for him, torturing prisoners?" My gut wrenches in disgust—making someone feel pain, except in self-defense, goes entirely against my indoctrinated warrior's code.

She rests her arm on her knee and looks out at the forest. "I was good at it. Too good."

I concentrate on my breathing, willing my voice to stay even. "You have regrets?" I have no idea what forms of torture she is versed in, but I am aware of some of the techniques the Ten Systems used during our war with them. If it's anything like it used to be, she has done horrible things. A terrible chill travels across my skin.

"Regret," she snarfs. "That's one way to put it."

"How would you put it?"

She turns vicious eyes on me. Her gaze is full of brutality, the kind I imagine she once used to force untenable amounts of pain on helpless beings. "I'm your enemy. Have you forgotten?"

"But you are not like him. You rejected him. You got away

from him so that you didn't have to torture people anymore." None of what she is saying aligns with who I know she is. The woman I have come to respect would not have made people feel pain just because she enjoyed it. There's more she is not revealing to me. My belief in her is not so easily diminished.

Her eyes widen with rage. "I'm worse!" She snaps it so loudly, it echoes around the forest.

"Assura," I say gently. "Whatever you have done, nothing you can say will convince me you are worse than Dargule. I know you far better than that." She was conscripted into the Ten Systems military. She would have had no choice but to comply with orders until she could escape.

"You haven't asked me," she hisses through her teeth.

"Asked you what?"

"How I knew to do those things to you. How I knew you would like the pain."

I did ask, and she said…well, she never really answered whether she had sex with the Ssedez or…

Wait.

"You didn't," I whisper, not believing the logical conclusion. "That's not possible."

"It is. I did." A slow, sadistic smile spreads over her face, as if to convince me she is evil. If I did not know her better, I would presume she is imitating Dargule. She must be pretending. I do not want to believe it.

My heart sludges to a murmur. What she's implying… That's not… I can't… "How?"

She shows her teeth like in a snarl, her gaze icy cold. "Ask me."

"Did you… Was he…" Oh gods, the full ramifications of what she's saying are pelting me in the chest. "You had a Ssedez prisoner?"

"Had? Still do." She points to the *Hades*. "Unless they've killed him in the six weeks I've been gone. After keeping him alive for a hundred years in a cell, I'd say that's doubtful."

I bolt to my feet and scream at her, "A hundred YEARS?"

Her eyes shift nervously. "That's what the Ten Systems does."

Fury like a branding iron burns across my skin. I go to the edge of the cage nearest the *Hades* and stare.

A hundred years...in a cell... "And you tortured him..."

"I did," she whispers so softly, I almost can't hear her.

I whirl back to her. "How fucked up are you?"

Her gaze drops to the floor. "Let me count the ways." She pulls her knees to her chest and wraps her arms around them, as though she's trying to be as small as she can make herself. The posture is one of guilt, of weakness, as I never would have believed her capable of.

I'm astounded and speechless.

"Fooled you, didn't I?" she rasps like her voice has gone hoarse. "I've fooled myself. Thinking somehow I could make up for it. As though the crimes I've committed could ever be forgiven."

She's right. Torturing one of my brethren should be unforgivable. Torturing anyone is a criminal offense.

She looks up at me, her eyes in shadow and her expression indecipherable. "Still want me now?"

I can't answer. Something between what she's admitted and what Dargule has accused her of doesn't add up to anything I have learned about this woman. There's information missing. She's not who she's making herself out to be. She's not telling me the full truth.

But the undeniable truth I do know:

I still want her.

My insides broil with the conflict of the hatred I feel for any human who would harm our kind and the desire I should never have had for her, which is as unquenchable as the need for air in my lungs.

I cannot sort it out enough to talk about it. I scrub a hand down my face. "We need to get some sleep if we're going to survive the *desidre* fever when the sun comes up. Obviously it's already taking effect."

She grunts something noncommittal and curls into a fetal position with her back to me.

I stare at her, disbelieving. The warrior-woman Assura I have come to respect seems to have disappeared. I retreat to the far side of the cage.

Her bitter revelation is for the best. I should be grateful. It will stop my body's forsaken urge to Attach to her, and I will continue mourning. She tortured one of my own kind. There is no circumstance, under any sun, where that should be forgivable.

Chapter Twenty-One

I sleep for as long as I can. Even after the sun comes up, I roll over and throw my hand over my eyes.

I don't want to see Gahnin. I don't want to look at him. I was right. I told him, and I've lost him. My covert attempts to help the prisoners survive, even as I was torturing them, don't matter, so I don't even try to defend myself by giving him that information. When I left with the rebellion, I abandoned them. I did not save them. They're still trapped on the *Hades* being subjected to the kind of pain I tried to save them from.

A seed of hope—well, not quite hope but obligation—starts in my gut. Those prisoners—I have to free them. Now is my chance. It wouldn't make amends for what I've done, but at least they'd be free.

It doesn't change that I was taking out my sadistic urges on Gahnin, either. Dargule, as screwed up as he is, was right. I don't know which I liked better—fucking Gahnin or digging my nails into him, biting him.

It terrifies me.

I left the Ten Systems to get away from that part of myself. I didn't want to be this torturer anymore. Turns out it's part of who I am, and I'll always be what I most despise.

But just because I leave the job doesn't mean I lose the instincts that made me so good at my work.

The hours pass, and the sun rises in the sky. Its rays seem to seep into my mind and blur my thoughts.

The burn begins. It starts as small flickers in my lungs then spreads through my veins. By the time the sun rages high in the sky, the heat isn't just in my blood. It's in my body, my cells, bursting within me, taking over every part of me.

Desire.

The *desidre* is here.

Guards and soldiers pass our cage, everyone watching us to see how we'll react to the fever.

With the burn raging through my veins, I don't care.

It starts as an ache between my legs. I ignore it for as long as I can. But it quickly turns to a throbbing, core-clenching need so deep within me, it's like my cells are crying out to be fucked.

I remember from experience—if I don't get myself off, it'll only get worse.

I reach between my thighs and find I'm soaked through my suit. One press of my fingers, and I moan with the excruciating need, the tortuous pain that is this place.

I'm having flashbacks, remembering how bad it got, and I want to cry with how much I'm dreading this. I can give myself an orgasm, but still this pain will only get worse as the day goes on.

I open my eyes and find Gahnin staring at me.

He sits across from me, his gaze a mask of heat and need. His fangs are elongated past his lip, and the eroticism of it is almost obscene. I stroke my neck just imagining what his bite might do to me. I don't know. But I'm dying to find out.

Then I see his hand. His fly open, he's stroking in languorous pulls. I need that more. He's hard and thick, a rigid column of gold flesh. My legs fall open, and I'm desperate to be filled, to have *that* inside me.

My fingers fumble with the buttons of the panel on my suit. I wrench it open and find my own flesh so swollen, my back bows on first contact with my skin. My fingers sink inside myself so easily, like slipping through cream.

And then I'm touching myself while I watch him fondle his cock, wishing like everything in every circle of heaven and hell that it was him instead of my hands sliding in and out of me.

But after last night, after what I told him, I'm doomed to suffer with my touch alone. He's too revolted by me, what I've done and what I'm capable of, to come near me.

It will be just like last time, except this time it will be worse. There will be someone in front of me who I can't touch the entire time.

I close my eyes.

I can't look at him anymore. It hurts too much, remembering just how good it was between us. How blissful it would be to spend the day feeding the *desidre* with him. Hours of nothing but sex with him.

I could happily die after such a day.

But it won't happen.

A climax builds within me, but I know it will not be enough. I try to make it last, because I know as soon as it's over, I'll just need to do it again.

My hands are pulled away. My thighs are spread by large firm hands, and…

"Ah!" The force of his thrust inside my body is an earthshattering entry.

But it feels so right. It's what I needed. His cock…it

moves in me like the center of my world. My body and every sensation spins around his fullness inside me. He moves in and out of me, driving, ever surging, as though pounding himself into me—not just his cock, but *him*.

His every thrust is a demand for me to feel his need. Like he wants me to be what he needs. Even though we both know I'm not.

I would do anything to be that person.

If I could erase everything I have ever done, all the traitorous baseless horrors I've committed, to be with him, I would. If I could change who I am, if I could remove the evil from inside me to be worthy of him, I would.

But none of those things are possible.

So I'll settle for being the sex his body demands.

His pelvis slaps against my clit, he's steel inside me, and I climax, my body clenching around him with all the heart-wrenching cravings inside me.

It's almost like the *desidre* doesn't create desire in me, it just releases every need I've denied every day of my life.

The need to be accepted. The need to be loved. The need to be valued and treated with respect. The need to be forgiven…

When it's just the sex, I can pretend that those things are possible. Him beating inside me, spurting and coming within me, pouring all the desire that lives inside him into me, he needs me, all of me.

But it's not real.

It's pretend, because it's only the *desidre* fever that has him touching me at all.

I don't care. I'll take him any way I can get him.

He finishes, but he's not finished.

He grasps me by the hair and pulls my face to his. He growls in a brutal clawing sound that's more animal than Ssedez, "Are you done?"

"No," I bite back. It's true. "I will never have enough of you."

His gaze is feral, saturated with the carnal need to fuck. "How much can you take?"

"Everything." I want it all, and I pray he never stops. I challenge him. "I can take more than you can."

The growl that vibrates from his chest is something wild. He twists my hair around his hand, and the sting of the pull is delicious.

I meet his stare, matching the carnal lust in his eyes with my own. "Give it all to me."

His eyes drift to my neck. He pulls my head to the side and fingers the column of my throat. He licks the tips of his fangs, and I can see the venom dripping off the tips.

I pull on his head as hard as I can. "Do it."

He shudders an inhale, and his eyes glaze over. Lightning fast, he strikes. His fangs slice into my throat, and I swear, I have died.

Exquisite ecstasy. Excruciating pleasure. It's not even an orgasm so much as a flooding of my nerves with the kind of feeling I imagine would happen if all the evil in the universe would wash away. Purity of feeling and white-hot bliss.

It quakes through my body and shatters my senses.

He is a drug. His bite is a high, and I never want it to end.

There will be no coming back from this. I will be addicted to him forever, yet never to have him again after this is over. I don't care. The thrill of having him now is worth the pain of losing him.

Time stops; my awareness ends. Everything blurs, and I can remember nothing but feeling.

He releases his bite, and I get on my knees in front of him, his cock in my mouth. I cling to it with my lips and tongue and teeth. I suck him until I'm feeding and choking on his come. Filling myself totally with him.

He shoves me to my hands and knees and speeds into me so hard from behind, I fear my bones will shatter with the sheer force and pleasure of it.

He leans over me, his chest molding to my back, and he bites me in the back of the neck. His hips bucking against my ass, his venom pours into my vein at the same rate he pumps into me.

I am overcome and thoroughly taken. He rules my body. I am the source and vessel for his desire. But it's not just desire. It's more.

It's *him*. He gives me everything he is and more. He bites me again and again. His venom fills me, transforms me, and makes my orgasms go on and on. I'm fucked every way I can be. His fingers and tongue in every crevice and hidden place. It's hours. The sun is far down in the sky when I get a moment's rest. I lie replete and sated.

Something I didn't think was possible in the throes of the *desidre*, but it's as though his venom takes the edge off. Like what his fangs give me is the best sort of *topuy*. Easing the fever and satisfying the ache at the same time.

I feel different, and when I lift my hand in front of my face…I look different, too.

My skin glitters in the sun's gold rays. It's pretty. It reminds me of his skin. It looks stronger, too, tougher.

Oh gods, that would be amazing. To have the armored quality of his skin. I let the fantasy run wild, imagining myself no longer vulnerable to a blade or a blaster. Imagining what that would mean in battle and how much fiercer and unstoppable an opponent I would be.

I glance over at Gahnin, who I expect to be sleeping with exhaustion. No. He's staring wide-mouthed at me.

"What's wrong?" I ask.

His eyes try and fail to stay on my face. His gaze keeps traveling down my body.

I chuckle, disbelieving, but I suppose, unsurprised, that he still wants more.

I sit up and run my hands down my naked breasts, my suit discarded somewhere long ago. "I'm ready for more, if you are."

He gulps hard and still can't take his eyes off my body. "Assura, I... You... Shit." He covers his face with his hands. "Gods, what have I done?"

Not understanding what he's upset about, I glance down at myself.

And gasp.

I am gold. Everywhere. It wasn't just the sun. My skin appears, for all the eye can see...Ssedez. He bit me so many times that I...

"Did your venom do thisss?" I jerk at the sound of my own words. I just hissed. Like a damn snake.

I lift my fingers to my mouth and feel my tongue—feel the twin tips, the thin dexterity of it. A surge of elation slips up my spine, wondering what else about me has changed. Wondering if maybe, just maybe...

I scratch myself. Nothing happens. No marks of any kind.

I do it again harder, and again, even harder. So hard that with my normal skin there would be at least red lines, even gouges or drawn blood.

Nothing. It doesn't even hurt. It almost feels...good.

Gahnin scrambles over and pulls my arm away. "Don't hurt yourself."

"Do you understand what this means?" I can't suppress my delighted smile. "Do you think I'm as strong as you now?"

His eyes widen in shock. "I, uh, do not know. Possibly."

I look around for anything that might have a sharp point. Something I could use to try to cut myself.

He leans to my ear and whispers, "There's a small knife hidden in the sole of my boot." He grabs it from the corner where it was thrown hours ago and uses our bodies to hide the weapon the guards never found.

He slips out the barest tip of the blade and holds my hand over it.

I press my hand down on it, to see if it can stab me. Nothing, no penetration. I bite my tongue to keep my sounds of excitement to myself.

I try to slice my wrist with it. Nothing. I try it harder and harder. It scratches, a slight white mark appears.

Gahnin whispers in my ear, "Pretend for a moment there's a blaster shoved in your back. You're inches away from being killed, and you have to use every ounce of your strength to save yourself."

I think the thoughts and let a trickle of fear through me. I don't want to die. I'll do anything to save myself.

My skin stays the same.

"Was something supposed to happen?" I ask.

His brows twist in confusion. "Maybe try thinking of needing to protect yourself and the person you love most."

That's easier. I think of Jenie. But it doesn't work. The white scratch is still there.

I try something else. I have an urge to think of someone else. I imagine Dargule pointing his electromagnetic shock device at Gahnin and when he knocked Gahnin unconscious yesterday.

And how much I would've given anything to jump in front of him and take the blow instead. If it hadn't been more likely to kill me than Gahnin.

A change starts on my skin. It thickens, and a tiny diamond pattern sprouts among the gold. "Ha!"

"Try it now," he whispers and there's a smile in his voice.

I try to slice my skin with the knife now. It doesn't even make a dent. "Wow."

He shoves the knife back in his boot and leans back.

"You are excited? You are not angry?"

"Why would I be angry?" I say, my glee irrepressible. "I'm impervious now. Think what that means? I'll never be ssstabbed again!"

A flash of horror crosses his face, and he reaches for my mouth.

But it's not to kiss me. "Open," he demands, pulling open my lips with his fingers.

I do. He fingers my changed tongue then lifts my upper lip to check my teeth. Which don't feel any different.

He lets go of me with a sigh of relief. "No fangs." But his tone is mixed, as though he can't decide if that's a good thing or a bad thing.

"Oh." It disappoints me. I can't return his bite and give him the same pleasure as he does me.

He sobers a bit. "I'm told by my commander it wears off in time and is not permanent, at first."

Another surge of disappointment. "Maybe I'll just have to make you bite me enough times so it is."

His eyes grow darker, and his fangs start to lower again.

I drag my hand up his arm and across his molded, chiseled chest. "We could start now."

A loud explosion, followed by dozens of shouts—in the direction of the *Origin*. Followed by the bright, flashing pings of laser shots being fired by dozens of blasters at once.

"An attack?" I stand and walk toward the edge of the cage.

The guards shout and point, moving toward the sound as well.

"Do you think your rebel friends left the safety of the Fellamana enclosure?" Gahnin asks.

"It's possible. I can't imagine Jenie just sitting like a duck for long when what's left of the *Origin* is vulnerable to Dargule's destruction at any moment."

"Or leaving *you* vulnerable to Dargule."

I shake my head. "She trusts me better than that. She knows I'm too good for him to conquer."

"Maybe you should believe it, too."

A blush, which likely won't show beneath my new gold armored skin, flushes over my cheeks. He's right.

"Your blade," I whisper. "Why didn't we try that yesterday to deflect the bars of the cage?"

"Because I didn't want to give away that I still had it when the guards were watching."

"They're not watching now. They're too distracted by the battle." It's the perfect time to get the better of them.

"Get dressed," he says.

"I don't need clothes anymore." I'm too proud of my new Ssedez qualities. I don't want to hide them inside a body suit.

"In case it wears off. You'll need them to protect your skin."

"Fine."

We put our clothes back on in silence, and he reaches toward the electro bars with his knife.

"Wait." I put a hand on his arm. "What if it melts the blade?"

"It might. But I doubt it. This knife is reinforced against heat, made to deflect fire the way the Ssedez natural armor cannot."

"Clever."

He chuckles and inserts the blade into one of the bars.

It works, cutting off the static. The source emanates from the top of the cage, not from the floor, so as he stands and raises the blade, it creates a hole, tall enough for me to step through.

But not wide enough for him to fit. His shoulders and chest are too broad.

"I'll steal a bigger knife from one of the guards and get

you out," I say, then sneak through the bars onto the dirt before he can propose a different plan.

I step out, and my ears immediately clear. My eyes fill with the distant trees around us. I shiver and shake off the static that's been a constant around my body since we were trapped in that cage. The guards are too distracted, and the noise of the battle is too loud to hear my footsteps on the ground.

I sneak up behind them, jab the first one in the vulnerable knee joint in the armor. He groans and sinks to his other knee. I steal his blaster, stun him, then aim for the other two.

My laser hits them both on the first shot in the gap between their helmets and the neck of their armor. All three are down and will be unconscious for hours.

I steal the knife from one of their belts and dash back to Gahnin. It's long enough to block out three of the cage bars.

All in less than a minute.

"Impressive." He steps from the cage and shakes away the feeling of static. "But you forgot." He pokes my skin, where it indents with his touch.

I forgot to will my natural armor out. "Damn."

"It'll become instinctive."

He rushes to the pile of our cached weapons, the ones we surrendered yesterday. But shots from blasters hit on all sides of us.

We turn, and Gahnin shouts, "Assura, your armor!"

I hold my breath and will myself to think about saving him. In my pause, a laser hits me in the forearm, and I feel…a little tingle. And that's it.

I guess I did it.

"No time to celebrate," Gahnin shouts, and tosses me my weapons belt.

But none of it matters.

Dargule walks out of the trees behind the soldiers

retreating to the *Hades*. He raises his arm and shoots us with the shock gun in his hand. A web of static wraps around my body, and the pain is excruciating. I scream, and I hear Gahnin do the same beside me.

The burn searing through my skin is nothing like the taunt of the *desidre*. This feels like I'm getting third-degree burns from head to toe.

I can't take it.

I feel my consciousness slipping.

Then, darkness.

Chapter Twenty-Two

Gahnin

The blast of an explosion rattles the surface beneath my ear. I raise my head to see Assura, lying on her side, her arms wrapped around herself, as though in pain.

A Ten Systems soldier stands over her, shaking her shoulder.

"Assura," the soldier says, trying to wake her. The voice is scratchy with a voice scrambler, but the person's posture, despite the shellskin armor, is curved over Assura in a caring way, with their back to me.

I look around and see walls of graphite gray made of some sort of metal. A loud hum starts to vibrate through the walls and crescendos. It's the sound of a starship rocketing from a planet's atmosphere into the vast void of space.

I grit my teeth as the sound grows louder, almost too loud to bear, then abruptly stops as we're released from the planet's gravity.

I'm a prisoner aboard the *Hades*.

But by the looks of this soldier attempting to wake Assura, we have an ally.

Assura's eyes drift open, and the soldier lets out a heavy sigh. Assura glances at the soldier's identification markings on her shoulder, and her expression brightens.

"Lennina," she breathes, her voice gasping.

There are wounds crisscrossing my skin from where the weapon burned me. I'm not used to wounds. I have rarely suffered them in my life. The pain is unusual and disconcerting.

I do not see any on Assura. I wonder if her Fellamana suit protected her better, or if the burns are beneath the suit.

The soldier unhooks her helmet and removes it. Her hair is short, cut at a sharp angle to match her jawline. But her expression is soft as she looks at Assura. "I thought I'd never see you again."

Assura tries for a smile but winces, still in pain. She's obviously worse off than me. Which makes sense. She may have my armor now, but she doesn't have the full Ssedez fortitude. Yet.

I have the urge to give it to her. As much as I have doomed myself even further by biting her, leading myself one more step on the path to a lifelong Attachment to her, I cannot stop the desire to do it again.

To complete her transition. I knew it was possible. My commander, Oten, did it with his new mate, but in the throes of the *desidre*, I could not think past the desire to bite her. The compulsion was too strong, even stronger than my reluctance to violate the sacred rite of the venom that is supposed to be reserved for the mated.

It's done. She's happy about it, so I refuse to feel guilt or regret. No matter how much misery it may cause me in the near future.

"I have only a moment." Lennina glances out the clear

front wall of our prison cell. "Dargule has called a meeting of the entire crew in the main hangar. In thirty minutes—"

"Everyone will be there?" Assura tries to lift her head in excitement, but she does not have the energy to sit up.

"Guards will be minimal. His egomaniacal tendencies are on a rampage more than usual now he's got you back."

"But there will still be guards on the bridge and security in every corridor, right? And the doctors in the medic wing—"

"No. That's what I'm saying. Dargule wants everyone to hear about his triumph and make sure we all know the rebellion is dead. He's insane. The bridge will be on autopilot. It's the perfect opportunity." She pulls something from her weapons belt and puts it in Assura's palm. "This will help you escape." A loud beep sounds in the corridor. "I'm sorry I can't help more."

She lifts her helmet to put it on.

"Thank you," Assura says.

Lennina shakes her head. "I should've believed in you and the rebellion. I should've left with you on the *Origin*. I've regretted it every day since."

"But if you had, you wouldn't be here to help us."

Lennina's lips curve in an almost smile. "The Freedom to Discover," she murmurs with religious sincerity.

"The Value of Life," Assura echoes her.

Like a slogan. Like a rebellious call to arms.

It must be the rebel code, the opposite of the Ten Systems credo to conquer and dominate every species and new world they find. Chills race down my spine, and I recognize for the first time what I did not before.

The *Hades* is but one ship in a thousand or more in the Ten Systems military fleet. Their might reaches all the known galaxies. And these women dared to rebel, Assura and her fellow crewmembers dared to escape—and succeeded.

The strength and skill, the sheer grit of will that would take…

I am awed for the first time, as I should've been from the beginning.

I understand better now what my commander Oten has been trying to convince me and what I did not fully believe: these women deserve our help. They should receive every ounce of assistance we can spare them.

Lennina snaps on her helmet and leaves, latching our cell door behind her.

Assura lifts what the other woman put in her hand. "Oh gods." Her face lights like she's just found a savior.

I move next to her, lying on the floor. "What is it?"

"I think…" She searches the device that has a tiny electronic screen and is no bigger than—

"Is that one of the shock guns that Dargule had?" I suck in an excited breath.

"I think so."

I take off one of my boots to test the shock gun on it. She drags herself over to the wall and sits up with it supporting her.

She presses one of the buttons and points it at my boot.

"Wait," I say and touch her hand.

"What?"

"Are there cameras in this cell?"

She looks immediately at the corners. "Two. There and there." She points at small holes in the ceiling that I never would have guessed contained lenses. "It's unlikely anyone is watching now, with the meeting Dargule called."

"But just in case." I put my boot back on.

"True." She lays her head back against the metal wall, and her breathing is too fast.

"We're going to get out of this."

She gives me a pained look. "I don't know how. I'm

useless. How are you healed already?"

"The Ssedez DNA learns. That's how we get our impervious qualities. My system remembers the first time Dargule zapped me with that thing. Eventually, I will likely become immune to it."

"No shit." She looks at me with wonder then glances at the ceiling. "That would explain a lot of things."

"What things?"

She gives me a side-eye. "You don't want to hear about the techniques I used on your fellow Ssedez."

I grit my teeth. "No." I did not need that reminder, either.

She sighs but changes the subject. "When the final meeting alarm sounds, you're going to have to escape to the bridge and seize control of the ship. There's a way from there to put the hangar on permanent lockdown, so none of the crew will be able to get out."

I glance at her neck. "There's a possible solution to your problem."

Her lips part, and her gaze goes to my mouth. "What?"

My heart pounds against my sternum, my pulse thundering in my ears. Biting her while I was in the throes of the *desidre* was… sacrilege but excusable. I was out of my mind with delirium, so I will not fault myself for it.

But my reason has returned. And yet I'm about to offer her my venom once more. I hold my breath to keep myself from saying it.

I have not bitten anyone since my mate died, and she is the only one I have ever bitten, the only one I have ever wanted to bite. Until Assura.

Her eyes are a warm amber, tinged with hope, the opposite from the guilt and shame she exposed last night. She's been extraordinary in her fight to escape and in seeing my venom and all it's given her as the gift for what it is. She is courageous, and determination runs through her veins thick as her blood.

The crimes she claims to have committed, she did because she was a slave to the demands of Dargule. There is more to her story than she has told me, and adding up all the truthful things I know about her, she is worthy of all the sacred venom I have to give.

But it is not about worth. It is about being my mate. Which she will *never* be.

For as long as Tiortan is in my memory, Attaching to one of the same species who killed her is impossible. Which means I have nothing to worry about. It doesn't matter that my body has physically Attached to Assura, or that I have filled her so full of my venom she is becoming like me. My soul will never Attach to her. I am not saving her life. I will never have need to save her life because she takes care of herself. The final two stages of the Attachment will never happen.

I have nothing to worry about.

Biting her now is about restoring her strength so that we can destroy Dargule. That is all it means. I let go the breath I have been holding and continue, "My venom will help you heal faster." My fangs are already descending past my lip, the venom pooling in my mouth at the thought of biting her again.

"In ten minutes?" she asks, breathless and staring at my fangs.

"Possibly."

She lifts her chin, revealing the smooth flesh of her throat, the pulse of her vein in her neck. "Do it."

My whole body crying out for the pleasure of biting her again, of feeling her mindless with the bliss my bite alone can give her, I grasp the nape of her neck and curl my other arm beneath her body. She is warm and soft in my hands, and I have a thought for getting her naked so that I can be inside her in nothing but her new Ssedez skin.

She clings to my arms and answers, "There isn't time," as though she can hear my thoughts.

She's right.

I lower my head and slowly, drawing out the moment, sink my fangs into her neck. She cries out and clings to my head. Her body starts to writhe, as in orgasm. It's almost the same and not the same.

For me, it's not so much orgasm as a deep-seated satisfaction. A relief and a release, a fulfilling of the desire to keep her, to make her feel so good that she is incapable of leaving me for any other.

I hold her there, my lips sucking on her skin while my venom pours into her.

Her body eventually calms, falling into the pattern of the ecstasy of the bite and accepting it. When I fear I may have given her too much, that the pleasure may have incapacitated her, I detach from her vein.

She strokes my face, her fingertips trailing over my cheeks and along my jaw. "Thank you."

My voice sounds hoarse, but I manage, "You're welcome."

Her gaze is filled with so many things, fascination, curiosity.

Affection.

It makes my heart beat faster. The part of my instinct that is Attaching to her screams, *It's working. She's returning the Attachment.*

I shut it down. It is impossible for her to return it physically, since no matter how Ssedez she may appear, she has not grown fangs as Oten's Nemona did. Without them, Assura can never bite me and return my venom.

I force the knowledge onto my brain. Perhaps if I believe that strongly enough, it will reverse the desire I feel for this woman of boundless passion, unlimited skill, and formidable strength.

Her expression closes down, her momentary vulnerability going back to wherever she hides it. She sits away from me, testing her limbs. Satisfied she feels improved, she leaps to her feet and bounces from foot to foot a few times.

She smiles at me. "Better."

"Good." I clear my throat and stand, not wanting to look at her too much. She's always been stunning, but with her new Ssedez qualities, she is so much like one of my own, it's confusing my body even more.

My instinct to mate is now shouting about what beautiful Ssedez babies she would make.

I rake my fingers through my hair and groan. *Stop.* If I could excise my thoughts from my brain with a blade, I would. *Must think casual.*

I put my hands against the front wall of the cell, the clear plexiglass, and wish we didn't have another twenty minutes to wait. Twenty more minutes locked up alone with her.

"Anewtan said something," Assura says behind me with hesitation. "I didn't think about it at the time. But…"

"What?" I snap and keep my gaze fixed on the wall.

"She said when your fangs come out, it means something."

I stiffen, afraid she's figured it out. Not that it would change anything, but I have no idea how she'll react.

"It means you just want to fuck, right?" She presses me to answer. "It doesn't mean that—like—"

I whirl on her and unleash all the conflict and frustration that's been broiling in me since I met her. This is her fault completely. The entire damn mess. "It means my body has decided to start forming the Attachment for you, okay? Does that make you feel good?"

"No." Confusion distorts her features. "What does that mean?"

I stalk toward her. "It means every instinct I have is telling me you're my lifelong mate."

Her mouth gapes, and I expect revulsion to come over her face. But it's the opposite. "Oh, Gahnin." Her voice is tender, and her expression is…

I can't look at her.

A force so powerful it almost knocks me over rears inside my chest. *She might return it. She has feelings for me. Compassion at least. Affection definitely. Possibly even love.*

"No!" I shout at the wall. Love is irrelevant, because I cannot love her. No matter how the thought sets off explosive protests in my chest.

She walks behind me and puts a hand on my arm. "Is it permanent?"

"Not until I attempt to save your life by sacrificing myself." Even then, it will be permanent only for me, not her. At least she will be safe from this misery.

Irony strains her voice. "Well, you'll never need to do that, so don't worry."

As if that's the worst of it. She has no idea how bad it is that it's come even this far. I whirl and get in her face. "I was supposed to be in mourning for another hundred years!"

She gasps and steps back, guilt filling her eyes. "I'm so sorry."

Something breaks in me. Something that lets go of the flood of things I keep bottled up and never talk about. "She was pregnant."

She jerks away. "Who?"

"My mate, Tiortan. When the Ten Systems blew up the civilian cruiser she was traveling on."

Assura covers her mouth with her hands. "No."

I have started. Why stop now? "We'd just found out. We had not told anyone." I kick the wall, and the metal *thunk*s from the impact. "I have only ever told one other person." Oten, my commander.

"Why?" she whispers.

"Her death was painful enough for the family. They didn't need to know we'd lost an unborn child, too."

"Why tell me?"

The rest of the dam in my fury breaks. "Because you need to know why it is impossible for me to ever mate with *you.*" I cannot hold back my sneer.

The hurt that clouds her eyes would prick at my guilt and my sympathy, if I did not know that my anger and hatred of all things human is justified.

"Because I'm human," she whispers. "Because humans killed…Tiortan and your baby."

I wince to hear her say it and have to hide my face. I should not have told her my mate's name.

"I understand," she says. "And I don't blame you for it. You have every right to hate me."

I lean my shoulder against the glass and do not look at her.

If I look at her, I might correct her.

Though I cannot love her, I am incapable of hating her.

Chapter Twenty-Three

Assura

I scratch my hand across my chest. It's a good thing he isn't looking at me. I've never felt so hurt before, and I'm incapable of hiding it from my face.

To learn in the space of a minute that he feels a mating bond for me, he lost a child in the war, and he is disgusted by my humanity and my past actions all at the same time—

My heart feels like it's been pounded flat then stuffed through a grater.

I stay huddled against the wall, staring at his back.

The worst part is the hope that flared inside me when he admitted his Attachment to me. I wondered for a moment what it would be like to live among the Ssedez. To live among a people who have never warred against themselves, who value their love for one another over any need to rule over other species.

To have a family.

I've never had one.

I was bred for the military by the Ten Systems. My parents were soldiers selected to procreate to make more perfect soldiers.

What must that be like to live among people who have chosen to be with one another for life? Who raise their children among them and take pains to protect one another?

What would it be like to live in such a place...with Gahnin? To never be separated from his constant sincerity and unwavering passion, or from his tenacious respect and quiet admiration? Or at least, I used to think he felt those things for me.

But hearing how much he has a right to hate me... I wonder if I imagined his respect, if it was ever real. If his attraction to me has ever been more than a biological demand to mate and an imperative to escape the pain of the *desidre*.

I murmur, wishing I didn't care, "Have you always been this revolted by me? Was the only reason you ever touched me because your instincts and Fyrian's atmosphere told you to?" I hold my breath.

"Yes." His response is tight, as though forced from his throat.

It makes water fill my eyes. I wipe it away. My heart shreds, but I disconnect from the pain. It doesn't matter. It's not like I ever felt more than physical attraction for him anyway. This is no time for sentimental bullshit.

We have a ship to commandeer.

The final gong goes off, the one that means the meeting has convened.

Numb to my emotional turmoil, I go to the latch on the cell door and hope the device Lennina left me does what I think it does.

I press the button, and a shock springs from my fingers, so powerful it melts the lock. The plexiglass door swings open. Gahnin moves in the corner of my vision. He's following me.

I don't have to look at him to know it. I don't have to see that look of disgust on his face again.

I snake my head out the door and look down the corridor. There's a guard on each end. I don't want to kill them. They're no more responsible for the evils of the Ten Systems than I was. They're just pawns, little better than prisoners, enslaved to the whim of Dargule.

I try for the lowest setting possible on the shock gun. The first shot isn't powerful enough to reach the guard. He turns to see me.

"Your armor," Gahnin says frantically behind me.

I grit my teeth, imagine saving his life—ignore the twinge of pain that thought causes me—and my skin sprouts the protective layer. The blaster shot the guard sends at me merely glances off me.

I turn the setting up on the shock gun one notch, and this time, the blast reaches the guard, and he falls, unconscious. I send the same shot at the other guard, and he goes down like a stone.

I race out of the cell, running full speed down the corridor, passing the cell block of all the other prisoners—each one whom I know intimately by name, body, and personality.

If we succeed, I can free them. My feet fly faster.

Or they do, until I have to stop. In front of Zeigan's cell. The tired and beaten Ssedez lies in the corner on the floor, his body so lax, his skin so pale and his limbs so meager, I fear he's dead. He resembles nothing of the formidable, golden Ssedez behind me.

I slap my palm on the glass and shout, "Zeigan!"

He stirs, and I breathe a deep sigh to see he is still alive. If barely. He turns his head and looks at us, his gaze hazy and delirious.

I reach frantically for the panel on the wall, the one with the controls to administer sustenance to the prisoner.

A small door opens on the wall of his cell, and Zeigan jerks awake at the sound. He's been conditioned to know it means water. He drags his body over to the dispenser and drinks from the bottle that appears.

"We'll come back for you," I say through the door.

He sighs in relief. "Assur... Thank you." His gaze widens on Gahnin, who is probably the first Ssedez he has seen since his capture over a century ago.

Gahnin echoes me. "We will return and free you." His voice is choked, and I wish we had more time. But the *Hades*'s crew will be closeted in the hangar with Dargule for only a short period of time. Our window is limited.

I grab Gahnin's hand. "We have to go."

He agrees and follows me. We race to the end of the hall and stop behind the cell block door. There's no way to see through it. We could open it and be meeting a trap. We could be racing into a horde of soldiers all holding Dargule's new shock guns.

We could be walking to our deaths.

"You cared for him," Gahnin whispers.

I glance at Gahnin, both of us breathing hard. "I shouldn't have stopped by his cell. We're wasting time."

He lays a hand on my shoulder. "But you did not have to stop and give him water. You led me to believe you tortured him."

"I did."

His expression is thick with confusion. "But he is still alive after so many decades. How?"

It was my job. I made sure they didn't die. I made sure they had enough to survive. I made sure no matter how sadistic Dargule's urges were, they would live to someday see their families again. "Many wished for death and hated me for not letting them die."

His expression softens, and he brushes my cheek with his

thumb. "You made it sound like you were as bad as Dargule. But you are not. You saved them, did you not?"

"I hurt them." I may have given them first aid, food, and water whenever I could sneak it, but nothing cancels out the torture I was forced to put them through.

He shakes his head like he doesn't believe me. Then he cups my face and kisses me.

I want to push him away and scream we have no time for this, but his lips meet mine and it's like that first time. Like I'm his shining, life-giving star. Like if he doesn't kiss me, he will stop breathing.

"Don't die," he breathes against my mouth. "I forbid you to die." His guttural tone holds the kind of authority that I bet even nature couldn't defy.

I shake my head. "I have no plans of dying. But I do have plans of saving. Let's do this."

He glances at the closed door again. "Dargule could be waiting for us."

"There's only one way to find out."

"I lied," he blurts.

"What?"

His gaze is vulnerable and thick with something far deeper than the desire I've become accustomed to seeing when he looks at me. "You are more than instinct and the *desidre* to me."

I gasp and stutter. "You...we...that's not relevant right now." But I can't stop the smile from creeping over my lips or the warmth his words spread through my chest.

He gives me another quick kiss. "Ready?"

"Ready."

He presses the button and the door opens.

Chapter Twenty-Four

Gahnin

Assura… I can feel my soul slipping away. Toward her. Or maybe it's swelling to include her. The very center of me, how hard I have fought to reject her and retain a piece of myself for myself, to not lose myself to her… I do not care anymore.

I knew there was more she was not telling me. I knew when she said she had tortured, it could not have been the whole story.

What I did not expect or realize and should have was how detrimentally, brutally selfless she is. What she must have endured to keep those prisoners safe and alive while under Dargule's command as they suffered from his cruelty daily…

She escaped him, and yet she came back here—to save them!

Then the door opens, and our worst fear comes true.

He's still outfitted in his black armor, his helmet removed. His soulless eyes glare at us with an emptiness that is more frightening than any rage or fury could be. He is utterly still, and his sociopathic urges are written all over his emotionless face.

Dargule laughs like the true villain he is. "I thought so. Who was it that helped you? I haven't fettered out the rat."

It sends a chill down my spine. It contrasts with the heat in my center, burning with the certainty that Assura's life is... so valuable.

Assura raises her hand to fire the shock gun, but Dargule is faster, already aiming at her.

I force her against the wall and shield her. Dargule's shock glances over my back. It burns, like fire seeping through my skin. I grit my teeth against the pain. One more of those, and I will be lying on the floor.

"Run!" I thrust Assura down the corridor, away from Dargule.

She pauses, confused.

"I can take the shocks, remember? My body has learned how to be impervious to them." Perhaps. Maybe. I have no idea what they will do to me, but I know for certain they will hurt her. "Go."

She knows where the bridge is. She knows I'm right. I can distract Dargule while she goes. I hold my breath, praying she'll do as I say, and that she can't determine the pain I'm in from the expression on my face.

"Don't die," she commands, then takes off at a full sprint, her long legs taking her faster than me and all my muscle could ever go.

I cover for her, stepping out into the center of the corridor, blocking Dargule from shocking her in the back with his gun. It works. He does not hit her.

He shocks me instead.

The static grips my whole body and short-circuits my nervous system. To keep from falling to my knees, I twist and lean sideways in to the wall, but I suffer with the satisfaction of knowing Assura will succeed.

Whatever happens to me is not important. She will live. No matter what species she is, no matter what her ancestors may have done to the person I loved most in this world, Assura must go on. Her survival is the only thing with any meaning to me.

"Did you think you could save her from me?" Dargule croons in his sickeningly sweet voice. "It would be better if you'd killed her."

I do not have time to answer. He shocks me again, and I see spots. The pain is worse than the last time, the electrical current burning hotter than before. Dargule has improved his toy.

"I made it so much more special," Dargule shouts maniacally. "A present just for you." The shocks rage through my nervous system, scorching my nerves, burning me from the inside out. This isn't something I can fight. He's going to kill me.

I realize too late what I've done by taking the fire for Assura. I've chosen to save her life—the final step of the Attachment.

I grasp the wall to stay on my feet and cling to consciousness, even as the pain threatens to take it from me.

My ability to love is not tied to some cultural tradition of mourning. To lose another hundred years—or even another hundred seconds—without loving Assura would be a crime against not just my own soul, but hers.

Dargule walks closer, his voice sounding nearer. "She's such a good little torturer. She does everything I say. Do you want to hear what I'm going to make her do next?" He stops beside me, his breath on my face. "Or should I say, who?"

I feel the Attachment thundering through my veins like a tide battering the shore. The need to protect her, the fear for her life. I know logically she can protect herself, but suddenly,

I don't care about anything anymore except making sure she comes out of this alive and whole. I have no feeling left in my limbs, but I react on instinct. A growl low and ominous resonates from my chest. I grab Dargule's arm and wrench it so hard, his titanium armor splinters like plastic, and his bone breaks with a vibrant *crack*.

He squirms in pain and tries to jerk away. But I already have his shock gun.

I press it to his throat, twist it to the highest setting, and squeeze the trigger. His scream is high and piercing and rings through the hall like beautiful music to my ears.

I pause the gun long enough to say, "You will never speak to her again."

He whimpers a pathetic sound of pain, and I hold the trigger down. The shocks course through his limbs until he is convulsing with seizures. His eyes roll back in his head, and his body goes limp.

Dargule falls to the floor with the hard *thud* of dead weight.

I breathe a sigh of relief and say a prayer of hope that Assura made it safely to the bridge. But I lose all balance and swerve against the wall. The shocks may have stopped, but the damage is done, my organs and sinews burned inside me. I fall to the floor.

Chapter Twenty-Five

I crash into a pair of guards who I knock unconscious in a one-two punch from my elbows. I run, the corridors eerily silent, and take the security lift up the three decks to the bridge and find it, unbelievably, unguarded. Seems like Lennina's information that everyone has gone to the hangar is correct. I get inside the bridge. I know why no one was exempt from the meeting to guard it. The panels and controls are all locked. A view of the stars and planets spreads wide before me in the viewing wall. I try console after console and am unable to gain access.

Shit.

I'm not a hacker. Computers are not my specialty. I have no idea what to do with them. But I can hot-wire. I know how to make electrical current connect and disconnect.

I shove my boot through a metal panel in the wall and wrench it off with the full force of my new Ssedez strength.

Inside, I start pulling at wires. I yank off a sharp piece of the metal and start cutting and rewiring things. It's a guessing game, but maybe something will work.

An alarm sounds on the panel by the large captain's chair in the center. I run to it and see a security question. One that is obviously for Dargule.

And one I know the answer to. It's the cell number of his favorite prisoner, Zeigan, the Ssedez. I know every one of the cell numbers by heart.

From there, it's easy. I check the security cameras for the hangar, and see every single crew member is there receiving instructions from Dargule's commanding officers for their new mission. I'm lucky that in this instance Dargule is such an egocentric control freak with a flair for drama, he insists on talking to everyone at the same time. The only people he excused were the prison guards, whom we already took out. And Dargule, who apparently decided to skip out on his own show to catch me…and Gahnin.

Gods, I hope he's still alive.

I enact the security lockdown procedure that secures the hangar entrances and exits. Nothing short of an atomic bomb that would destroy the entire ship will be able to open those doors now. Except me, from the captain's chair.

The entire crew is imprisoned. They cannot get out. No idea what we'll do with them, but for now, they're out of harm's way.

I halt the ship's engines and pull up the communicator. I record a message for Jenie, letting her know what I've done, and send it to all frequencies on the Fellamana planet. Someone will get it to her.

Then, I forage for weapons and arm myself, blasters on my hips, knives in my belt. And jackpot—I find two of Dargule's favorite new toys in the compartment beside his chair.

I pull up the security cameras and double-check all the

corridors to make sure no one skipped out on Dargule's meeting. Every camera comes up empty of people. Everyone is too afraid of Dargule's punishments to disobey his order to be in the hangar. They're all trapped there.

I flick to the camera feed I really want to see, on the level where I left Gahnin to fight Dargule. The first thing I see is Dargule lying on the floor, unconscious.

But I can't rejoice.

Gahnin is lying beside him.

I secure the unconscious Dargule in a vacant prison cell first, to be sure he can't wake up and attack me while I'm helping Gahnin.

Gahnin, his big body lying bent, is unconscious but breathing. He must have been hit hard by the shock gun. Hard enough to knock him out, but he should wake up in a moment.

I wait, one minute, two, and he doesn't.

I start to panic.

What if Dargule shocked his brain somehow, and his mind is—

"Gahnin!" I shake him. "Wake up. Do you hear me?"

He doesn't respond, does not move at all. Panic builds in my chest, and my palms begin to sweat. I have no idea how to give a Ssedez first aid. I cannot lose him. I've only just met him. Only just found out that he likes me, sort of.

He sacrificed himself for me. My heart pounds, and my eyes sting. He did it despite his rightful hatred of me, despite what I've done, despite what humans did to his mate, despite knowing what could happen to him if he risked his life for mine. He could have completed his Attachment. For me.

I should feel guilt. He should never have to give up his

mourning for his mate, for anyone. But even with all that, I can't stop myself from thinking—if he comes back, he might be mine, forever.

I don't know what's right anymore. If it's better for him to live or die or if what I'm vainly hoping should be impossible; all I know is, he cannot die. I won't let him.

Then…I feel them.

Against my lip. Something protruding from my mouth.

I lift my fingers and gasp, feeling the sharp points.

I have fangs. They're not as long as his, but they're there with a strange-tasting liquid dripping into my mouth. My gums ache, and the sight of Gahnin's bare, vulnerable throat ignites an instinct in me.

I want to obey it. But…how can it possibly work?

His skin is impenetrable.

He was able to bite me, though, after my skin changed. I have to try.

I strike, and my fangs slide into his neck with an ease I never would've guessed. I feel the venom slide from the tips into his vein, and the relief comes from a place so deep inside me, I have to moan.

I sink my fangs in as deep as they'll go, until my lips meet his skin, and something else happens.

A fullness, a rightness starts in my chest, a kind of completion, like the laws of nature and my existence have finally met and molded in perfect harmony. Like my body and its desires have physically joined with my heart as tightly as a yin and yang.

And it's with Gahnin. I have to wrap my arms around him, to hold him as close to me as I can. I want to care for him and protect him and love him and never stop.

I want this feeling forever.

I want him, forever.

A groan sounds from deep within his body, and he stirs

back to consciousness, and his hands come to my head, holding my bite as close to his skin as he can. His hips start to writhe as though in arousal, and I feel it within myself, too.

The need to have him inside me, to be one with him, to make love to him, is like a lit fuse within me.

I reach for his cock, not caring where we are or who might be watching, but he palms my cheek and stops me. "Wait." His breathing is ragged and out of control.

"What?" I can barely think around the drive in me to mate with him. It's untenably strong, as fierce as life and death. It'll physically hurt if he forces us to stop. His fangs are out, fully descended and hard as steel behind his leather. I don't understand why he's stopping me.

He fingers the spot where I bit him on his neck. "Do you know what you have done?" he says with shock and wonder dripping from his tone.

I'm pulsing from my heart to my lungs and every ounce of blood coursing through me with the need to be with him. I force myself to breathe. I don't know what it is I've done, but it's bad. Something about me biting him back has stirred a life-altering response.

He presses his hand over my heart. "Do you feel it?"

His palm against my chest brings only a sliver of the closeness I want to feel with him. I want to merge with him— body and soul. If I have to let him go, it would be like cutting off a piece of myself. It's as though I have become Attached to him.

I gasp in horror. "No."

He eases himself to sitting in front of me. "Yes." His hands wander over my shoulders and down my arms, as though he can't stop touching me, and his touch is reverent. Like I'm precious. Like I'm worth an extraordinary value I didn't know I possessed.

"The Attachment…" I whisper. My voice feels balled up

in my throat, like no sound wants to come out.

"The Attachment," he echoes. His eyes brighten, his wonder blazing into something stronger. Something with his whole heart...

"Don't love me," I blurt.

He strokes my cheek with his fingertips and smiles, "Why not?"

"Because I'm not...because you can't...because..." I don't know what I'm trying to say. All I know is that this is impossible. "I'm not lovable!" It comes out bitterly childish and coarse, like my emotions and feelings have overwhelmed my ability to form cohesive thought. I don't know how to explain myself.

"Of course you are lovable, Assura." He presses a delicate kiss to my forehead. "There is so much about you to love."

"No, no. No, no, no, no. No." I push his hands away, not wanting to be touched. Well—my body is raging with the need to be made love to—by him. But it terrifies me so much, I don't want him touching me anywhere. I might say *to hell with it*, and just do it without thinking or remembering that this is all messed up, twisted and wrong.

A pain slashes across his expression as though my rejecting his touch is a physical blow. "Assura, please." He reaches for me. "This is the way it is supposed to be. This is what you and I are meant for. This is not something you can refuse."

"I'll refuse anything I fucking want to!" I jump to my feet. I don't want to look in his face. I don't want to hear him tell me what I can and can't do. "I did not sign up for this. If I had known that biting you would do this, I..." I choke, afraid I'll lose it and cry. I can't believe I forced him into this.

"You what?" he snaps, standing in front of me. "You were just going to let me die? Without your venom, I would have."

"You weren't...I don't know. You might not have actually

died." I sound ridiculous. Like a stuttering child, making excuses.

He stares at me hard, both eyes drilling into me. "We both know there is no scenario where you would have willingly allowed me to die. Do not deny it."

"You could have warned me!" I scream. "You could have told me that biting you would be another step in making this permanent! Then I would have at least made the choice. Now… now…" My voice cracks, and I turn away from him. I don't know what's happening to me. I don't know how to walk out of here without him. Who am I without him?

He is me and I am him—we are one and the same.

Fear, harsh and stormy, comes over his face. "You are refusing me…" He swallows hard, and his fangs, as I watch, begin to retract into his mouth.

"Of course, I'm refusing you. My people killed your mate and your unborn child. We slaughtered them in a brutal genocide. I tortured one of you." I point toward Zeigan's cell in the next room. "There is no scenario in the universe where you and I should ever be together."

His upper lip curls, and a snarl breaks from his throat. "Those are my problems. Not yours. You have yet to give me one single reason why *you* are rejecting *me*."

I inhale to reply with no words.

He's right. Those are all reasons why he shouldn't be able to love me or form an Attachment to me, and yet here he stands, ready to commit to us. "Why?" I breathe in disbelief. "How could you possibly consider having *me*?"

Sadness turns down the corners of his mouth. "Oh, Assura, do you not know?"

There is nothing he has to say that I want to hear. "No, I don't. And I don't want to know. You're the one who should be asking what you don't know. What things I've done, you can't fathom. The horrible crimes I've committed. I was

Dargule's number one for years. You have no idea what he made me do. If you knew, you wouldn't be standing here. You never would've touched me."

He gapes, stunned. "I care not what you have done. I know you."

I shake my head. "You're blinded by the Attachment. By chemicals and hormones poisoning your blood so you can't think straight. If you were in your right mind, you would never want me, let alone love me. You didn't lie to me before. Your attraction to me has been only chemical from the start, and that is all it will ever be."

"Assura…"

"You don't know me! You can't love me!" No one can. No one should. I don't want them to. I back away from him.

"Please do not do this." Agony contorts his features, as though seeing me leave causes him physical pain.

I feel it, too. Like a raking of my heart over hot coals and a rupturing of my internal organs. Like I'm defying the laws of physics and, once I leave him, I will no longer exist in space. As though he is the air in my lungs and the blood in my veins. I will die if I am not with him.

I leave anyway.

"Assura! Assura!" he shouts after me. The anguish in his voice rings through the doors and echoes into the bowels of the ship. It pulls tears from my eyes.

This may kill both of us. But I can't be his, and I have no right to call him mine.

Chapter Twenty-Six

GAHNIN

She does not look at me or speak to me all day.

She focuses on freeing the prisoners. One by one, she opens their doors, feeds them, clothes them, comforts them, all by name, each with murmurs of support and assurances that they are liberated and will be reunited with their families. And that they never have to see Dargule again.

Assura refuses to look at Dargule.

It is left to me to restrain him when I discover he is still alive. I ask Assura if I should kill him, and she ignores me as if I am not there. I cannot tell if it is because she does not want to talk about Dargule or if she does not want to talk to me.

So I chain him in his cell and check on him often.

I function, somehow. She is functioning, some way. I glimpse her alone on occasion and see the misery on her face that she is trying to hide from the others. It matches the suffering I feel within myself.

I know now that even Tiortan, as tender and compassionate as she was, would have forgiven Assura for whatever crimes she was forced to commit, for whatever things her species has done to others. Assura has more than earned her redemption, if she ever needed it to begin with. She chose to hurt people herself so that Dargule wouldn't harm them even worse. She made it as bearable as possible for them, all the while planning a way to help them escape.

Assura is so wholly lovable, she becomes more so to me every hour I watch her. The only problem is that she cannot see this about herself. She does not know how good she is. How empathy is so embedded in the marrow of her bones, no one could doubt it, no matter how she tries to deny it.

No wonder she cannot accept my love for her. Or even believe I could love her. She sees only the pain she has caused and not the good she has done. I wrack my brain for how to help her forgive herself and see herself as worthy of being loved.

My body longs to do it physically. To make love to her until I have touched her soul and wrapped it in ecstasy so she can feel how much I love her. Though, with our history, I'm not sure any amount of lovemaking would help. It would probably make it worse, reinforcing her belief that my Attachment to her is only physical and not emotional.

We've been awake for twenty hours, tending to the freed prisoners. I'm exhausted, my body drained from fighting the Attachment burning through me, from denying the need to be immersed within her permanently.

I see her digging through a storage closet for clean uniforms to give to the prisoners, and I glimpse her mouth. Her fangs are out, the little tips gleaming white extended past her bottom lip. It's an intensely erotic sight that has my cock swelling on instinct. I cannot see her fangs and not think of her biting me, of the exquisite pleasure of feeling her pierce my skin and share her venom with me.

She closes the closet and stops, staring at me. Her breathing elevates. I expect to see revulsion or for her to immediately run from me. Instead, she drags her gaze over me, her eyes resting between my hips. Her delicate twin-tipped tongue snakes out to lick her fangs, like she's thinking of tasting me, of taking me in her mouth.

A laugh sounds from the other end of the corridor and startles her back to the present. She shakes herself and turns away from me, but stumbles.

She catches herself, but not before I reach out to help her. I grasp her upper arm, and she groans. I assume she will pull away, but she does not. Disbelieving she's letting me touch her, I stroke her arm, the feel of her warmth in my hand, the sound from her throat seething with lust and need.

It reminds me of the discomfort she must be in. It's been hard for me, and I've been a Ssedez for over a century. I have endured the pleasures and tortures of the mating bond before. For her, newly formed fangs, new to the mating bond, new to anything else that she may be experiencing because of my venom, her body is under siege.

"Let me help," I whisper.

She shivers and starts to walk, away from the others. I follow. I will not leave until she tells me to go. She turns a corner and comes to an alcove, then grabs me and shoves me against the wall.

I have no time to breathe, no time to think if this is a good idea, no time to ask if *she* thinks this is a good idea. She tilts my head and buries her fangs in my neck.

My moan of pleasure and gratitude rumbles through my chest so loudly, I wonder the entire ship does not hear it. But I do not care. I wrap my arms around her, and I soak in the bliss of feeling her body against mine, of having her lips sealed to my skin as she pours her venom into my vein with her precious fangs.

I comb her back, wishing I could peel away her clothes and feel her naked, skin flush with mine, and sink inside her and never leave. She writhes against me, the apex of her thighs rubbing me, and I have to bite my tongue to keep from coming.

She reaches a hand between us and wraps her palm around me, stroking me, as if I needed to be any harder. She detaches her fangs from my throat and hisses with her sweet tongue in my ear, "I'm going to *sss*suck you off."

I swear and watch in awe as she retracts her fangs and descends to her knees. I don't understand why this is happening or care what the consequences may be. All I can think of is seeing her mouth stretched wide and the tip of my cock disappearing between her lips.

She fumbles with the fly on my leathers, her hands shaking in urgency, and I help, my rigid gold flesh freed and distended. She swallows me to the back of her throat, her jaw stretched and wide, trying and unable to take all of me. I pant heavy breaths, the pleasure of her hot, wet mouth so exquisite. Her hands stack on the shaft, stroking and twisting; her tongue laves and lathers the tip, salivating.

I will not last, not with watching her and feeling her at the same time. To see her, this human who I have come to love like she is one with me, in front of me, pleasuring me so—amid her rejection of me—it fills me with hope. Maybe she has changed her mind. Maybe this is her giving in to us.

Or it could be the opposite. She could reject me again when we're done. She could be doing this only to alleviate the sexual agony of the Attachment in the moment. I do not have the will to stop and find out.

My body throbs with the need to be inside her, and my gums ache to bite her. My Attachment instincts do not care what her motives are. I want only to make her come.

I grip her hair and pause her head. "Are you ready for me to fuck you now?"

Her eyes meet mine, her lips swollen and wet from sucking on me. "Yes*sss*."

I grasp her shoulders, pull her to standing, and twist her back against the wall. I look down at her waist, at the material shielding her luscious cunt from my view, and hiss in gratitude. She's still wearing the Fellamana suit with the "fuck panel."

She pulls open the buttons. I wrap her thighs around my waist and drive inside her.

I growl at the pleasure and the agony—the heaven of her tight heat gripping my cock, the hell of not knowing if she will let me stay here, of not knowing if this will mean anything to her.

I pause, buried to the hilt inside her. My hips pump convulsively, unable not to move within her. "Let me...love you," I groan in her ear.

She wrenches at my hair and growls, "Shut up and bite me." I do not need to be asked twice.

I strike, hard, fast, my fangs penetrating deep into her neck. Her resounding cry is so sudden and abrupt, I worry I have hurt her, but she holds my head to her neck, fingernails digging into my scalp.

"Don't stop...don't stop...don't stop." She breathes in litany and grips me so hard with her thighs, squeezes me so hard with her cunt, I am gone.

Primal and unbridled, I pound her hips like a piston, a machine of need unable to slow or lessen. All I can do is keep going and going and going. In and out of her. I gnaw at her neck and thrust inside her like the ravaging animal she makes me become.

My purpose in this world, my whole existence, depends on making her come, on filling her with everything that I am, and driving her so insane with the ecstasy I make her feel, she's incapable of rejecting me again.

She holds me like it's true, clings to me as though if I ever let her go, she will die with the loss. Her incessant sounds, her orgasmic cries, her incoherent sighs break through my fears and wrap around my heart as though each one is a declaration for more of us and a withdrawal of her refusal.

I want to hear it in her words, though.

After she's come more times than I can count, and at a lull between my orgasms, I retract my fangs and kiss her, her mouth a succulent haven made for tasting and exploring.

"Be with me." My words sound hoarse and guttural. "Be mine."

She freezes, every muscle in her body going rigid, her softness and surrender at an end. Alarms go off in my head.

I swear and cling to her. "Please, Assura. What this is between us is—"

"Just sex," she snaps and pushes at my shoulders. "Get off of me."

I do, but slowly. I slide out of her, and she shudders at my withdrawal, little whimpers of longing. This one time is not enough. The lust still raging between us from the Attachment is not something that can be satisfied after even hours of sex. It would take days, weeks. And now that she is Ssedez, her body would be able to withstand everything she craves.

"If it were just sex, it would not be like this."

"I can't, Gahnin," she moans. "Please let me go." Her arms push me away, but she folds toward me as though her mind and body are at war, unknowing what it is she wants.

"You want me; I know you do. You are growing to love me. Why do you fight it?"

"Because I don't know who I am when I'm with you." She breaks away from me, and the absence of her, the loss of her touch feels like I've lost a part of myself.

"I know who you are."

Her eyes clench shut in confusion. "If I don't know who I am, no one can."

"Then help me to know. Let me help you to know."

Her chest heaves up and down as though just breathing is a labor.

Encouraged, I step closer. "We can figure this out together. You do not have to suffer alone."

She glares at me, a barrier of defensiveness shielding her expression. "I don't trust you." She bends down to pick up the pile of uniforms and stalks away down the hallway.

Her words are a fist to my gut. Seeing her walk away, all of me still desperate to have her back, to touch her and never let her go.

She is right. She has no reason to trust me. She did not ask for this mating bond, and I did not warn her. She should have had the choice, and I robbed her of it. I don't know how we ever come back from that. How can I ever expect her to accept a bond that was forced on her?

I cannot.

Which means...I have lost another mate before I ever learned to know her.

Chapter Twenty-Seven

I finish my rounds checking in on my freed prisoners—I have to think of something else to call them. I don't think I can call them my friends. A jailor can't become the captive's friend. That's not how it works.

The physical pain I feel being separated from Gahnin beats through my veins and aches in my core. I would weep if I could, but I'm too exhausted from just resisting him to cry. I'm still damp between my legs—from all his copious amounts of come. It's even more than before. The mating bond must make it worse.

I should shower. I should clean up. But I don't want to let go of the reminder of him inside me. Of him making love to me. It's what he makes it feel like. The brutality and near violence of him fucking me should be just that—a fuck. But it wasn't. I could feel it as though in the center of my heart how much he wants to love me. With every thrust and drip of his venom into my veins, it was like him drilling home how he cares for me.

But I don't trust it. I don't trust him. I don't trust myself. If he knew, really knew me and what my life has been like with the Ten Systems, he would not feel those things. No matter if it's a biological mating bond. He doesn't know me. The Assura he thinks he loves does not exist.

Besides, I have more important things to worry about.

I need to find a way to communicate with Lennina and get her out of the hangar. She's still trapped in there with the rest of the crew. I've checked on the security system multiple times, and they are not getting out of there. We have to figure out what to do with the crew. Some of them will probably declare allegiance to our rebellion, but the rest…

I'm too weary to solve any more problems today. My heart and soul feel like they've been slaughtered, and I can't move another step. I collapse on a bed in an empty officer's quarters, too wasted with emotional pain to tap the control to close the door.

I close my eyes and let myself feel all the life-changing things flowing through my body. It's like my nervous system is on hyperdrive, like every inch of my skin is so sensitive and desperate for touch—his touch—I have no idea how I move forward from this, how I go about living a life without him in it.

"Assura."

I bolt up at the sound of his voice. "Gahnin?" Forgetting in my weakness that I've sworn not to speak to him. Gahnin is at the door, but it's not him who said my name.

The recently released Ssedez stands in the doorway, gaunt and wearing Ten Systems uniform pants. His chest is covered in scars, many of which I gave him. Just to see him makes my stomach twist in revulsion and disgust—not at him, at myself. At what I have done and can never make up for.

"I hope you don't mind," Gahnin says gently. "I thought

Zeigan might like to talk to you." His expression holds more compassion than I deserve. I can't look at him.

"Fine." I turn my attention to Zeigan, and Gahnin leaves.

"I am sorry to intrude," Zeigan says in my language.

I clear my throat. "How are you feeling? Do you need something?" I try to remember what I've given him—food, water, clothes, a bed, medicine, I think. Or was that someone else? My brain is so fogged from the Attachment, I can't remember.

"I am well enough. Thank you." His gaze catches on the window on the wall, of the view of the solar system, and he gives a pleasurable sigh. "I have not seen anything but the inside of a prison cell in a hundred years."

"You'll never have to see the inside of a cell again." I try to be positive and not dwell on my guilt of not being able to free him years ago. It took me too long.

"Assura…" he murmurs, and there is a note of awe in his voice. "May I come in and speak with you?"

"Um, sure." I stand up from the bed on shaking legs and gesture toward the seating area of straight-backed chairs. "Please sit."

He shuffles in on shaky legs, one dragging more slowly than the other. I remember when I broke that leg a year ago, how Dargule forced me to shatter Zeigan's kneecap with one of his fancy torture devices that was similar to a hammer.

He catches me staring. "It will heal, now that I can get proper medical treatment." He sits, slowly, gingerly.

I intended to sit beside him, but I can't. The shame inside me is like a vapor poisoning my lungs. "I'm sorry."

He gives me a sensitive smile and points to the chair beside him. "Please, sit with me."

My lungs seizing around the air, I do. But only because he seems to want me to.

He reaches for my hand and holds it gently in his. I have

to bite my lip to keep from losing it. His gentleness is more than I deserve. "You are remembering when you broke this leg." He nods toward his deformed knee.

I try to speak, but my words are stuck in my throat. I can only nod.

He squeezes my hand. "Do you also remember saving it?" I can't answer, I do remember, sort of. "I would have lost the leg entirely to infection, probably died from it, if you had not snuck me the antibiotics." He points to a round scar on his chest, the one where I stabbed him with another of Dargule's brutal toys, so many times it left a scar, though it never completely penetrated his Ssedez armor. "Do you remember this one? How you whispered, I'm sorry, I'm sorry, the whole time, and told me to scream louder so that Dargule would let you stop?"

I try to agree, but all that comes out is a hiccup.

He points to a jagged scar along the length of his bicep. "You won't remember this one."

"You had that when I met you," I mutter.

"I had many torturers before you. Do you know what they were like?"

I nod, then shake my head. "I knew some of them. I... tried to make sure it was me and not them who Dargule picked."

"You did." His expression is so warm and tender, I have to turn away. Kindness is not something I can accept. "You saved us, Assura."

I clench my eyes shut, determined not to let the relief and pain his words inspire come spilling out in tears.

"You came back for us," he whispers. "You freed us."

I can't take anymore. I know he means well, but all his words make me want to do is wail and scream about all the horrible things I've done. About how it doesn't matter how much I tried to make up for it, it doesn't change the fact that

I still hurt him.

I take back my hand and stand away from him. I go to the window and stare at the stars. I force out the words with a tight voice, straining not to cry. "Thank you, Zeigan."

I dread what he'll say next, but instead, I hear the chair scrape and footsteps going out the door. I sigh with relief and lean against the glass. Zeigan left.

But my relief is very short.

"You can tell me." A different deep voice sounds from the door.

I stiffen and cringe. It's not Zeigan this time. I know that voice.

"What do you have to lose?" he continues, his voice moving closer inside the cabin. "What is the worst that could happen?"

Anger rises thick and furious in my gut. I turn to yell at Gahnin, scream at him to leave me alone. But the words stop in my throat. Gods, look at him... He is not only the center of my world, and the axis around which my life turns; he is the sexiest, most erotic vision I have ever seen. He is...

My mate.

I clench my fists and growl in my chest. I won't give in to it. This godsdamn mating bond has to go. Now. "You knew what he was going to say, didn't you?"

"I had no idea. I just assumed it was something you should hear."

My lungs tighten. "You should go."

He sits in the chair where Zeigan was and crosses his legs, like this is a leisure occasion. "Tell me your worst. Scare me away. Let us get this over with." His expression is a mask. I can't tell what he means by it.

His eyes flash with a thrill of expectation. "I dare you to disgust me. If you can."

My upper lip peels back in a snarl. "You can't handle

what I did. You'll run screaming like a baby."

"That is what you want, is it not? To get rid of me."

I meet his gaze and stare down his challenge. He's right. If I want to kill this mating bond he feels for me, I can.

He leans forward. "Do it."

I want to. If I tell him the truth, it'll kill his delusions that he could ever love the real me.

I inhale and start with Zeigan, every injury I caused him, every twisted sick thing Dargule forced me to do to him. Gahnin's reaction isn't the revulsion I expected. He's still blank-faced, but I don't stop there. I go through each prisoner, in order of their cell numbers, and what tortures I put them through: the guts and the gore, their blood on my hands and their screams in my ears. Every single malevolent thing I did to them.

But as I go and go, minutes bleed into an hour, more, and I lose track of why I'm doing this, what my actual goal is. I forget to care about Gahnin's reaction and just keep talking and talking with this never-ending need to be heard.

I pace and stay on my feet for as long as I can, but my anger wanes.

My energy fades, and I sit in the chair across from him.

"Did you want to do it?" Gahnin asks quietly.

My whole body revolts, "No." A whole new desire of other things I need to say forms in my chest.

He nods encouragingly, and my words change from scare tactic to confession.

I divulge my struggle to make sure it was me and always me that Dargule picked. The sick things I did to prove I was the best at making the prisoners feel pain, so that Dargule wouldn't pick one of the other guards, one of the true psychopaths. I describe how Dargule punished me when he thought my torturing wasn't severe enough, how he sometimes tested his new toys on me first.

I start to run out of words. I reach the end of stories to tell. "I didn't want to do it," I whisper, staring at my hands, my fingers shaking and my pulse pumping in my ears. "I *hated* it."

There's silence, my will for words at an end. My chest feels empty, like I've dumped my heart out and realized there's nothing left but this vacant hole. The guilt and the shame... I don't feel them anymore. It feels more like pain, now. Like fear.

The shaking that was just in my hands spreads to the rest of my limbs, and I feel it—the sheer terror that I lived with every day. The fear of Dargule killing all of us. Of watching everyone around me die one by one, and being left alive—being the only one for him to take out all his sadistic urges on.

I shake so hard, my heart racing, I double over and fall toward the floor.

But Gahnin dives ahead of me and catches me. He wraps his arms around me and holds me. He presses my head to his chest and cocoons me in the sheer strength and muscle of his arms and body.

My shaking lessens, and I take a heavy breath against him.

He rubs my back. "You are safe with me now."

I gasp and cling to him. I wrap my arms around his neck so tight, I never want to let him go. There's something else in my chest, something inside the emptiness. Something warm and begging to be let out.

"I love you," I blurt before I know what I'm saying and hold my breath. Just because he's telling me I'm safe doesn't mean he still wants to be mated to me. But now I've started, I have to tell him how I feel.

He cradles my face in his hands and looks at me with adoring tenderness. "You do?"

"I couldn't say it before. I was too scared." And I don't

care that tears are finally running down my cheeks. I don't want to stop them, because I want him to know. Everything. I don't want to hide anything from him anymore. "I was afraid you'd find out what I'd done and leave me."

"My love—" His voice breaks, desire consuming his gaze and tightening his mouth. "You are the bravest person I have ever met."

A bright moan of joy escapes my lips. "And you love me, even knowing all of it?"

"I do. I love all of you, everything you have endured and everything you have done to survive. To save the people Dargule imprisoned, you took the worst burden upon yourself. You sacrificed so much, because you're good. It makes me love you more."

I can't help laughing a little, disbelieving what I'm hearing. "I'm sorry I pushed you away. I was just so afraid that—"

"You have nothing to be sorry for. You do not have to be afraid anymore. I am here for you. Always."

I take a shuddering breath, wishing I could breathe in his words and hold them inside me.

He moans, "Assura," and kisses me. His hands cup my face, his lips mold to mine, and everything I've been desperate to express to him pours from my mouth into his.

"Gods, how I love you," I hear the words sneak from my mouth when I breathe, unsure if he can hear them.

But he does. He buries his tongue so deep in my mouth and twines it so tightly around mine, it's as though he wants me to express everything I feel for him and more.

It's too much and never enough. The empty place in my chest, the vacant one where all my guilt and shame were stored, feels warmer. Like he's filling it, like if I could inhale enough of his kisses, he would heal every broken place inside me.

"I'm sorry I forced the mating on you," he whispers against my lips. "I should have warned you it could happen. I should have confessed my Attachment to you sooner and explained to you how it worked so that you would have a choice."

I grasp the nape of his neck and smile. I was in the Ten Systems military; I remember what it was like to have no choice. This is so very, very different. Attachment or no, every cell in my body would be crying out to stay with him, even if I were still fully human. "I have two feet. I could walk away. You haven't chained me." But the thought of the one time he did put me in chains has heat spreading low in my body. "Though we could play that game again sometime."

"Not if I beg you first." He threads his fingers into my hair and devours my mouth with all the fervency I need. His palm strokes down my neck, and I feel his fangs descend into my mouth.

I suck on them, tasting the sweet syrupy venom. He pulls my body against him, wraps my legs around his hips, and he's hard, rubbing through our clothes, contacting me in the place where I am aching to have him inside me, needing him filling me. All of me.

I pull at his leather waistband, my shaking fingers desperate to have him.

He undresses me, lowering the zipper of my suit. His hands glide over my chest and my arms, savoring the feel of my skin, loving the feel of me.

This is real. He loves me—the real me and everything about me.

There's another piece of it, something else I'm afraid of, but there's nothing that could make me interrupt him. I need this too much. My body and my heart are crying for this. I feel his every touch, his every kiss down to my soul, like a balm to heal all my wounds.

"I almost forgot something," he whispers and stands.

My body aching with the loss of him, I watch him press the button and close the door. It eases something in me, and I understand.

Privacy. The luxury we have never had.

"Are there cameras in here?" he asks.

I shake my head. "Not in an officer's quarters." I should probably figure out who it belongs to—someone locked inside the hangar, but they can wait a little longer.

A blissful, sensitive smile bends his lips. "We're alone. No one is watching."

"No one is watching," I sigh. After how many times, with no choice of our own of being watched, it is heaven. This is between him and me. It is only us now.

No one can take that away from us.

He comes to me and lies me back, removes his clothes, and rests his body against me. We are gloriously naked and skin to skin, as though in a bodily communion.

He trails his lips down my chest and sucks my nipples until I'm squirming from the pleasure it ignites in my core. He dips his hand between my thighs and sinks his fingers deep within me. From his lips clasping my nipple to his thumb on my clit, the simultaneous stimulation sets me off.

Since the mating bond awoke in me, the orgasms are unlike anything I've felt before. Even with the *desidre*. Or with his venom.

A lightning through my senses, filling my brain with ecstasy that shoots off like sparks and drives climactic waves through every corner of my body—that never retreat.

He lifts his mouth from my nipple and sinks his fangs into my thigh. His venom pumps into my clit and the swollen opening where his fingers thrust in and out in a torturously slow rhythm.

He replaces his fingers with his mouth, and I feel worshipped and adored. His tongue and lips like soothing fire, burning away all my pain and guilt with pleasure and love.

Then he is over me, his chest against mine, and his cock buried inside me.

I cry out and cling to him, pulling him in deeper, ever deeper, begging my body to take as much of him as I can hold.

He urges my mouth to his throat and whispers, "Please."

I'd almost forgotten my new fangs, which are protruding and aching from my gums. I strike, and he groans so hard as my venom pours into him, his body seizes in climax.

He loses his control, and his carnal desire, the animal instinct to obey his body's visceral need to mate, overtakes him.

He pounds into me, his pelvis ramming against mine, setting me off again. My mouth goes slack, my fangs slip out of him, and he returns my bite, pouring bliss into my vein as his hot come heats me from the inside.

He orgasms, again and again, and the bliss of him, the pleasure of being what he wants, what he needs, combine with the trust of knowing he has committed to me. This is forever...

I freeze beneath him. Something's not right. Something inside my head. Something he doesn't know. Something I've forgotten to tell him.

He pauses over me. "What's wrong?" he asks, breathless, his gaze hazy with lust.

"I..." I push him away. "Stop."

He pulls out of me, leaving drops of his come on my thighs, and shifts to my side. "Did I hurt you? Was I too much?" There's a thick fear in his voice.

I put a hand on his chest to ease him. "No, no. You're perfect."

He covers my hand with his and kisses me. "Tell me, my love, what is it?"

My love.

Gods. I have to close my eyes to soak it in.

I never thought I could hear someone call me that who wanted me for their own—for life. I would've thought before it would make me feel confined or restricted. But not with him. It makes me feel...free. Free to be loved and valued in every way.

"There was a part of me that liked it," I blurt, still unable to open my eyes to look at him. "As much as I tried to make it easier for them, I liked manipulating the torture techniques. I didn't like making them feel pain but..." I swallow, trying to put this need of mine into words. "I liked controlling what they'd feel. I don't know if I always liked it, or if I learned to like it because Dargule made me do it so much. But I did."

I open my eyes to stare at his chest and whisper, "I still do." I shudder to admit it, but I can't hide this from him, or myself. I am not a coward. I meet his eyes. "The way I dug my fingers and teeth into you before—the way I used the knife on you—I want to do that again." I flex my fingers against his gold skin, watching his flesh give beneath my nails, and I want to do it harder. I want to inflict all my urges on him, to have him experience the things I want him to feel.

He deserves to know. Before he really agrees to this, he needs to know that I'm not wholly good, the way he is.

But there is no revulsion on his face, only love, even... desire.

I don't understand that at all.

He runs his thumb along my lower lip, grazing my fang. He stabs his thumb on my fang and then drags it across the tip.

I gasp and look down at his thumb. "What did you— you're bleeding!" Red dots trickle in a line over a cut from my fang on his skin. "My fangs can cut you?"

He nods. "And if you'll notice, I liked it." He presses his

hardness into my thigh, so I can feel it throbbing against me.

"How is that possible?"

"Ssedez fangs are the only thing capable of penetrating our skin. It has to be that way or our bite, our venom, the pleasure of it, would be useless."

It makes sense. I'd never thought of that.

He holds his thumb up to my mouth again. "Now, lick the cut."

I run my tongue over it, swallowing his blood, and shuddering at how much I like the taste of the coppery drops. But when I take my tongue away and look at his thumb again, the cut is gone.

"The tongue, the saliva, heals it," he says.

"Wow."

"What I'm saying is…" He puts his mouth to my ear and whispers with a seductive rasp, "I want you to make me bleed."

It makes me flinch how much I want to. "Are you sure?"

He closes his eyes and nods slowly, emphatically. "Please."

I'm in disbelief that this could be possible, that I could find someone to love me—all of me, even the vindictive parts of me. "Really?"

He opens his eyes and implores me. "I'm begging you."

"I love you," I blurt, unable to not say it again.

"And I love you." He cups my cheeks. "But are you going to deny me? However much you want me to beg, I'll do it."

That makes me smile. I think I might like that, to see him on his knees, begging me to hurt him. "Maybe next time."

I run my nails down his chest and flick my fangs across his skin, admiring the red cut I make.

He moans and rolls to his back, urging me on top of him. "You can do that to me forever."

"I will."

Chapter Twenty-Eight

Gahnin

She pleasures me with her fangs, until I'm so raging with lust for her, I have to bend her over the bed and fuck her until she's so full of my come, it's dripping down her thighs and onto the floor.

Then we do it again.

The mating frenzy has begun. It usually lasts a week or more. Among the Ssedez, we would be given quarantine, time alone for days to satisfy it, with nothing to do but eat, sleep, and make love.

But alas, we have a ship to run and ex-prisoners to care for. We're incapable of leaving the bed for the rest of the day, but we eventually have to leave our precious privacy.

We help Lennina escape from the hangar, along with three other crew members sympathetic to the rebellion. They're so relieved to hear Dargule is in prison, they demand to see it for themselves.

I send a message to my commander, Oten's ship en route

to the Fellamana planet with repair supplies for the *Origin*. He arrives at our ship the next day and boards with his new mate, Nemona.

She and Assura stare at each other for quite a while. It's uncanny, seeing two human women who have been turned Ssedez next to each other.

Nemona holds out her hands to Assura. "Congratulations."

Assura grasps her hand, too. "For what?" I'm surprised there isn't more affection between them, but I understand better how much intimacy was between Assura and Jenie that did not occur with all her human crew mates.

I'm also surprised Assura does not understand what the congratulations are for.

"Your mating!" Nemona smiles knowingly at her.

Assura's smile in her golden face radiates. "I guess it's obvious, isn't it?"

Oten puts a heavy, sure hand on my shoulder. I hold my breath. This is where he'll judge me for ending my mourning for Tiortan a century early. Not that his opinion would change anything.

He tries to speak. "I am—" He has to cough to get through his words. "I am overjoyed that your mourning is over, my friend."

The relief his words bring relaxes a tension I did not know was in my chest. I don't know what to say. He puts two hands on my shoulders and looks at me with many inexpressible things. "I will tell everyone it is a miracle and something to celebrate that you did not have to endure another hundred years of loneliness." He knows about my private pain of losing a mate and a child. He knows the torture it's been for me for too many decades longing for this to happen again. He does not judge me for ending my mourning sooner than is traditional. "Your mating is a momentous thing for you."

I am unable to not embrace him. "Thank you."

He pats my back and murmurs a phrase in Ssedez, "When the heart is full, life is fuller."

I tell him about the Ssedez prisoner Assura has done her best to care for. We update Nemona and Oten with everything happening on the ship.

"Have you heard about the *Origin*?" Nemona says heavily. Whatever it is, by her tone, it sounds bad.

Fear widens Assura's eyes. "What?"

"The *Hades* bombed her, destroyed her as it was leaving the planet. Everyone is okay, but the *Origin* is gone."

Assura gasps, and her eyes fall closed. I wrap my arm around her shoulders.

"Do you have plans for what to do next?" I ask.

"Well." Nemona crosses her arms. "We've got the *Hades* now. I think she deserves a re-naming and some renovation, but she's the best at stealth, and her defenses and weapons can't be beat. We could do worse."

Assura nods. "We have to figure out what to do with the rest of the crew."

"Some will join the rebellion; some will not."

Nemona's gaze remains serious on Assura. "What do you want to do with Dargule? He's your prisoner."

I know what I'd do with him: hang him by his toenails and poke at him for days, weeks, make him bleed and suffer all the tortures he's inflicted on so many others.

Assura does not answer, her eyes round and considering.

"We can execute him," Nemona offers.

Assura shakes her head. "Don't kill him. Not yet. We need to find out what information, if any, he has sent back to the Ten Systems about us."

"Very true. You're right."

"In fact..." Assura bites her lip, then a vindictive grin curves her mouth. "Let the other prisoners have him. Zeigan and the rest should determine his fate."

I squeeze Assura's shoulder, and Nemona nods agreement. "Done."

"As for us." Assura glances at me. "I'm wondering if we could have a leave. Some time to just…" She hesitates as if not knowing what to say.

"Be?" I offer, stroking her cheek. "You have been through a lot. You deserve some rest."

She gives a slow smile, and her eyes soften. "I do."

I look to Oten. "Commander, I ask for official leave for a new mating." It is customary in the warrior's code to receive from two weeks to a month for such an occasion.

Oten nods, "Permission granted. You may take my light cruiser and return to our planet to be near your family, if you wish."

Nemona adds to Assura with a blissful smile, "The Ssedez planet is beautiful. Filled with restful, peaceful people." Her gaze is filled with a longing. "We'll be visiting often. Go."

I'm conscious of the fact that Oten and Nemona are only a little over a week into their mating and have received no such leisurely leave. "Commander, do you—"

"Nemona wants to return to her crew," he says. "We'll have our reprieve at some other time in the near future." He glances at her like this is an agreement he is holding her to.

"Yes," she smiles. "It can't come soon enough."

Assura and I do as Oten offers and leave for my home planet within the hour.

Once off the *Hades*, the relief in Assura is visible. We stand in a viewing window on Oten's ship as we float away from the *Hades*, watching the ebony starship fade into the distance.

"I don't ever want to be on that ship again," she says.

I caress her back. "You don't have to. The only thing you have to do is be with me." I touch her chin and urge her eyes away from the ship she loathes and onto me. "If you choose."

"I do choose." She returns my affection. "I choose to become your new family. Whatever ceremony the Ssedez require to do it, I want it."

My heart, if it was full of my feelings for her before, spills over in a way I never thought it would again. That is the only ceremony I need. "You already are."

Acknowledgments

Writing about hot aliens on a sex planet would be nowhere near as fun without the support of so many.

Thanks to my wonderful editor, Tracy Montoya, whose attention to detail has made this story come alive in ways I could never manage on my own. To the encouraging marketing and editing teams at Entangled Publishing, and to my champion in battle, my agent, Rachel Brooks.

To Bronwen Fleetwood—there is no value I can place on your unwavering support. Thanks for your ever-present empathy, your tenacious skill and your tireless knowledge about how novels are built and assembled!

To my writing group—PWG—every week you remind me that this work is fun and that telling stories is always better with friends around to listen.

To my buds with #RWChat and the New York City Romance Writers, who make the insanity of romancelandia the sanist place to be.

To my husband, who's taught me what it feels like to be loved, who's given me the endless need to capture on the page what love feels like in real life. I fall short every time, but I'll never tire of trying.

And…thank you for reading, readers! For going on this wild sexy adventure with me. Reach for the stars and never settle for less than the very best you are worth. XO

About the Author

Robin Lovett enjoys trips to alien worlds to avoid earthly things, like day jobs and housework. When not reading romance with her cat, she's busy writing sexy books, which may or may not involve anti-heroes, aliens, or both, but almost always enemies-to-lovers. She's a big fan of her husband who regards writing romance as far more important than practical things, like paychecks. Her favorite surprise in the world, or the universe, was finding out by some miracle other people want to read the same kind of stories she loves to write. You can reach her on Twitter @LovettRomance or on Facebook @LovettRomance to chat or share ideas about what to put in the next story.

Discover the **Planet of Desire** *series*

TOXIC DESIRE

DREAMING DESIRE (COMING SOON)

If you love erotica, one-click these hot Scorched releases...

Sin and Ink
a *Sweetest Taboo* novel by Naima Simone

Being in lust with my dead brother's wife guarantees that one day I'll be the devil's bitch. But Eden Gordon works with me, so it's getting harder to stay away. I promised my family—and him—I would, though. My days as an MMA champion are behind me. But whenever I see her, "Hard Knox" becomes more than just the name of my tattoo shop. Surrendering to the forbidden might be worth losing everything...

Good Girl's Bad Lessons
a *Dirty Debts* novel by Carmen Falcone

Translator Emma Cavanaugh will do anything to win her ex-boyfriend back—including summoning her brother's best friend, Italian billionaire and playboy Nico Giordano, to give her much-needed lessons in the art of seducing and pleasing a man. Sex was never her thing, so if anyone is going to know how to teach her how to be bad it'll be Mr. Sex-on-A-Stick himself.

Snatched

an *Outlaw Warriors* novel by Cathleen Ross

Hellbent on revenge, Club Enforcer Troy DeLance kidnaps his prospect's sister as payback for a betrayal. If he has to tie Stacey Martin to his bed to make her stay, so be it. All the better if she likes it. Stacey will do anything to save her brother. Even surrendering in ways she never imagined to her beastly kidnapper. But as their relationship heats up, neither realizes someone else is plotting a more deadly payback...

Rescued by the Space Pirate

Part One of *Ruby Robbins' Sexy Space Odyssey* by Nina Croft

Ruby Robbins has always dreamed of going to space. So when she's approached to help her country—by going undercover in an alien slaver ship—she jumps at the chance. She never expects her biggest challenge will be fighting off a sexy space pirate determined to save her. Or that she'll enjoy the struggle quite so much...

Made in the USA
Columbia, SC
10 September 2021

45273507R00145